Farley, Steven.
Wild spirit / Steven Farley. --New York : Random House, c1999.
121 p. --(Random House riders)(Young black stallion ; 4)

975001 LC: 98067189 ISBN:0679993592 (lib. bdg.)

1. Horses - Juvenile fiction. 2. Horses - Fiction. I.

(SEE NEXT CARD)

Suddenly, from the direction of the upper pasture came the sound of Redman's piercing whistle. Raven turned his head and froze. Redman called out again.

Is that a welcome? wondered Danielle. *Or is it a challenge?*

As if answering her question, the colt called back. Now there was no question. This was definitely an unfriendly exchange. In fact, hostile was more like it.

Raven uttered another shrill scream, and his ears swept back flat against his head. Seconds later, the two horses were galloping madly toward each other. In a few strides, only fence rails would be keeping them apart!

Danielle's heart froze. A gasp caught in her throat.

"No!"

BOOKS BY WALTER FARLEY

The Black Stallion
The Black Stallion Returns
Son of the Black Stallion
The Island Stallion
The Black Stallion and Satan
The Black Stallion's Blood Bay Colt
The Island Stallion's Fury
The Black Stallion's Filly
The Black Stallion Revolts
The Black Stallion's Sulky Colt
The Island Stallion Races
The Black Stallion's Courage
The Black Stallion Mystery
The Horse-Tamer
The Black Stallion and Flame
Man o' War
The Black Stallion Challenged!
The Black Stallion's Ghost
The Black Stallion and the Girl
The Black Stallion Legend
The Young Black Stallion (with Steven Farley)

BOOKS BY STEVEN FARLEY

The Black Stallion's Shadow
The Black Stallion's Steeplechaser

Young Black Stallion

4

Wild Spirit

Steven Farley

Random House New York

To Melly Lingo

A RANDOM HOUSE BOOK

www.randomhouse.com/kids

Library of Congress Catalog Card Number: 98-067189
ISBN: 0-679-89359-8 (trade) — ISBN: 0-679-99359-2 (lib. bdg.)
RL: 4.5

Printed in the United States of America
10 9 8 7 6 5 4 3 2 1

Contents

CHAPTER ONE

Home at Last

Danielle Conners smiled as she walked beside her horse. "Good boy, Redman," she said soothingly. "That's my guy. Just a little further until we get there, okay? It's time to go home."

The big red paint bobbed his head sleepily. The two of them had been stuck in a cramped horse van almost all day and all night. *It sure is nice to finally stretch our legs a bit,* Danielle thought.

The sure-footed sounds of Redman's hoofs clip-clopped along the straight dirt driveway.

"Has this all been a dream or what?" she asked her horse. "It feels like only yesterday when you were at Mr. Sweet's riding camp in North Carolina and I was throwing snowballs in New York. But now we're both back, safe and sound, in Florida!"

A pickup came up behind them and passed through the main gate of the South Wind Thoroughbred Training Center. The driver waved to Danielle and leaned out of the cab. "You're sure about walking the last stretch home?" he asked.

"Positive. Reddy and I haven't done this walk together in a while," Danielle answered.

"All righty. Enjoy yourself," said the driver as he pulled off.

Danielle and Redman watched the truck rumble away. Suddenly, Redman twisted his head and tugged on the lead line. Something was moving in the trees on the other side of the road.

"What is it, boy?" Danielle gazed in the direction Redman was staring and laughed when she saw two blue jays rustling in the bushes. "It's just some birds, fella. That's all."

The two of them continued along the county road that led to the Conners farm. Looking back over her shoulder at South Wind, Danielle saw the long barns and part of the training track. Her gaze followed three horses galloping out to the far turn of the track. The training facility was a busy place.

A crisp, familiar breeze blew in Danielle's face. It helped to wake her up a bit, since she was still exhausted from the long van ride. She closed her eyes and breathed in the smells of her horse and home. It had been quite an adventure. But the important thing was, now she had two whole weeks during the holidays to spend with Redman. It was definitely worth it.

As the wind whistled through the trees, Danielle remembered how Alec Ramsay had been the key to the whole deal with Mr. Sweet. Without Alec's help, Redman would still be in North Carolina. Fortunately, there had been room enough in Alec's horse van for Redman to hitch a ride home.

In the sunny green pasture to the left side of the road, a few cows looked up from their grazing to watch them pass. Danielle's gaze drifted toward Redman's back. She was dying to jump on and tear through the pasture as fast as they both could go.

Get a grip, she told herself. *There will be plenty of time for that later. We need to get reacquainted first.*

Redman glanced at Danielle expectantly with large eyes.

"I know you're hungry, Reddy," she said. "We'll get you some breakfast as soon as we're home. Then we'll get rid of those shipping bandages."

Danielle hadn't given much thought as to how she would get Redman *back* to North Carolina after the two weeks were up. Mr. Sweet had left that decision to her. But Danielle knew that she would come up with something. In the meantime, the most important thing was that Redman was home. It was the best Christmas present she could possibly have asked for.

Danielle reached out and gave the paint a big hug. "Oh, Reddy, I missed you so much," she said.

"We'll go out to the river and to the marl pits and Gator Grotto." Redman swished his tail back and forth.

Danielle looked up at the sky. "Feels a little different than yesterday, doesn't it, Reddy?" she asked.

The air was a bit cool, but it was a much warmer Friday morning than it would have been in Rocky Mount, North Carolina.

Tramping along the straight stretch of road, Danielle began to think about all the comforts of home, like pouring a nice big glass of milk from the kitchen refrigerator. She also started to wonder how much Redman would remember about the farm. Would everything come back to him when he saw the familiar barn and pastures? Would he recognize all the sights, sounds, and smells?

Alec Ramsay had warned Danielle that some things might have changed. For instance, he'd told her Redman might not remember parts of his life at the farm that Danielle hoped he would. If only she could be sure that her horse was as glad to be getting home as she was to have him back!

At last Danielle saw her family's house behind the big oak trees that partially hid the farm from the road. *Redman has to know where he is now,* she thought.

Redman began to snort with excitement, rapidly switching his tail. *He does! He does know!* Danielle told herself as she tightened her grip on the lead line.

Though her home would always be "the farm" to her, Danielle knew that it really wasn't much of a farm anymore. Since Redman had been away, Raven, Alec Ramsay's colt, was the barn's only resident. Now that Raven was at South Wind for a few days getting examined by the vet, the paddock and fields were entirely empty. It was the perfect time for Redman to come home.

Danielle checked her watch. It was mid-morning, so her mom would probably be at work.

She led Redman straight to the barn for his breakfast. *He must really be hungry,* she thought. Like the rest of the horses in the van, Redman had been fed very lightly on the ride down.

As they stepped into the barn, Redman sniffed the air. He looked around intently as if searching for something. "What is it, boy?" Danielle asked. "Do you smell Raven? He's not here, fella. But you smell him, don't you?"

She led the big paint to his stall, undid the latch on the door, and walked him inside. Then she brought him a couple quarts of oats and took his water pail to the faucet outside the barn. When she returned, instead of placing the pail in the corner, she held it as Redman pushed his muzzle down into the water. Danielle's fingers touched his mole-soft skin as her horse drank greedily. She softly hummed a gentle tune that she thought would ease Redman back into his old surroundings.

Finally, Danielle left Reddy to eat in peace and ran toward the house. Her mom had left the kitchen door open and she quickly poured her long-anticipated glass of milk. But it was impossible not to think about Redman. She grabbed some carrots from the bottom shelf of the refrigerator and hurried back to the barn.

Redman was just finishing his light breakfast of oats and hay. He was nosing around in his feed trough, licking up any stray kernels of grain he could find.

"Here you go, big guy," Danielle said as she broke off a few pieces of carrot.

Redman crunched down on his dessert, then murmured a whispery neigh. Danielle led him out of his stall and clipped the cross-ties to his halter. Moving from leg to leg, she set to work undoing the shipping bandages. Then she headed to the chest in the tack room for the brushes and the currycomb. She was about to close the lid when she saw Redman's old blanket folded neatly inside.

She ran her hand across the rough material, recalling how she used to bury her head in it to breathe in the lingering smells of her horse after he was taken away from her. She wouldn't have to do that any longer. *Well, not for two weeks, anyway,* Danielle reminded herself.

She left the room and quickly set to work grooming her horse. Redman shifted his weight as she brought the brushes across his body. Whenever he moved, Danielle moved with him. She stepped back beside Redman's rump and started brushing the straw out of his tail. Glimmers of light shone in the paint's eyes.

After giving Redman's coat and mane a quick brush, Danielle stooped to pick up his feet. She worked from hoof to hoof, cleaning out the dirt and manure that was packed within. When she finally straightened up again and stood next to Redman's head, she saw that the light in the paint's eyes had brightened to a sparkling shine.

Taking a cloth from her pocket, Danielle ran it first along her horse's neck, then over his body and down his legs. When she had finished, she led Redman into the paddock, opened the gate to the lower pasture, and turned the big paint loose. He hesitated a moment, then glanced at her with his lips curled.

"It's all yours, big guy," Danielle said, gesturing toward the sprawling field. Redman neighed for joy at the sight of the waiting pasture. Then he set off toward his playground of green grass, his tail flying high.

Danielle felt like flying, too. Her horse was home at last!

CHAPTER TWO

Back on Top

Redman broke into a canter and swept across the field. Danielle climbed up on the wooden pasture fence to sit and watch. She still couldn't believe her eyes. Her very own horse was back!

As she sat atop the fence, Danielle thought about how differently Redman moved from the new colt, Raven. Raven had grown so much in the past few months that he was nearly as big as Redman. But he seemed to have only two speeds: fast and faster. He tended to run in dizzy fits and starts, zigging and zagging, his heels flying. Redman's style, on the other hand, was just the opposite. Each movement was deliberate, with no wasted motion at all.

The big paint kept cantering along, midway up the low-rising hill and across the field. He ran to the fence, then stopped to gaze out over the trees and woods beyond. He stood still for a moment, as if remembering. Then he trotted off and continued his tour. He gave a snort and came up the field, stopping in front of Danielle. His neck was arched, his head cocked a little to one side.

From her perch atop the fence, Danielle reached out to touch Redman's tousled mane. Then she ran her hand down his satin neck. Almost before she realized it, she had slipped lightly from the fence onto his back. It felt completely natural.

Redman moved forward without bolting. His gait seemed effortless and easy. In no time at all, the big paint broke into a gallop, and Danielle slid forward, pressing her hands close to the sides of his neck.

Wow, Danielle thought. She had forgotten how high Redman carried his head, even when he was in full gallop. In fact, it startled her just how much she seemed to have forgotten about riding the horse who had always been such a big part of her life. Still, some things could never be forgotten, like the familiar touch of her knee to his withers and the feeling of power that was greater than her own.

Redman's strides swallowed the ground, and he swerved abruptly to avoid a tree. Danielle caught her breath and moved with him, reveling in the glory of his smooth and fluid movements as he leveled out again and went back up the field.

"You're the best horse I'll ever know," Danielle told him. "I've missed you so much since you were gone. If it hadn't been for Raven, I would have gone completely nuts." She gave her horse a warm pat. "Wait'll you meet him, Reddy. Little Buddy is really special. You'll see."

They were at the far end of the field when Danielle saw Alec Ramsay's pickup wheel through the driveway and pull to a stop beside the house. Danielle's older brother, Dylan, hopped out of the passenger side and headed for the kitchen door. Alec climbed out the other side, walked over to the paddock fence, and waved. Danielle waved back and started riding toward him, easing Redman slowly into a bouncy walk.

Just then, two motorcycles came racing up the county road past the house. Their motors roared loudly, startling Redman, who was still charged from his run. Danielle felt her horse hump his back beneath her as if wanting to buck. Suddenly, he bolted!

Danielle slid backward as Redman's swift move caught her unprepared. *Don't panic,* she told herself. She quickly reached behind her to find Redman's quarters. Her right leg swung over Redman, and she slipped off, landing upright but staggering backward.

Redman ran a few paces and then slowed to a walk again. Snorting, he shook his head and lowered it to graze.

Feeling a little embarrassed, Danielle glanced back toward the fence by the paddock. Alec was still standing on the other side. She walked closer, and he called out, "You weren't ready for him, Danielle. That's the way you get hurt."

"I know," she told him as they met at the fence. Eager to change the subject, she asked about the van load of fillies they'd just delivered to South Wind.

"They're all fine," Alec said, "even Darsky." The black filly had scratched her leg on the trip down from Aqueduct. "Henry's happy, too," he added, referring to Hopeful Farm's head trainer.

"I was sort of wondering there for a minute," said Danielle. "Henry sure didn't seem happy when he saw Redman in the van." Henry had given her and Alec an earful earlier that morning. He was really mad about Redman's catching a ride in the van that also carried *his* champion fillies.

Alec shrugged. "It's hard to tell what Henry's thinking sometimes. Mostly, it's what he's *not* saying that you have to worry about. But we managed to get all the horses down here okay, so he can't complain too much."

Alec looked a little sleepy. He was still wearing the same clothes he'd had on last night, jeans and a tee-shirt, as was Danielle. She glanced down at the wrinkles in her own shirt. Her mom wasn't going to be impressed. Danielle needed a shower, too.

Alec turned to gaze at Redman, who was playing in the pasture, tossing his head and dancing around. "Redman doesn't seem any worse for wear," he said. "He's certainly full of zoom."

"Almost like a different horse," Danielle said, smiling. "But he *is* still the same Reddy, all right."

"It'll be interesting to see how he and Raven get along," Alec said.

Danielle nodded. "They'll be friends. I just know it."

"Well, I wonder about that, Danielle," said Alec. "Raven's not like those fillies Redman was hanging out with before, you know. He's reaching that age when..."

They both turned as they heard something coming along the road. A large horse van turned into the driveway.

"Well, it doesn't look like we'll have to wonder much longer," Alec said. "Here comes Henry with Raven now."

The silver-paneled horse van began dipping and weaving as it eased over the bumps in the long driveway. Above the strain of the engine, Danielle heard the thud of hooves inside the van.

"You'd better get Redman away from here, just to be safe," Alec said. "At least until we get Raven unloaded." Danielle nodded and led her horse to the upper pasture. She quickly turned Redman loose and hurried back to the paddock.

The van came to a stop in front of the barn. Danielle could see Henry sitting in the driver's seat, wearing his usual cap. He switched off the ignition and swung down from the cab of the van as Alec went over to meet him. Danielle jumped the fence and ran up behind them.

"So how'd it go?" asked Alec.

Henry nodded. "Fine. Gene says that Raven's feet are in first-class shape. The vet gave him his shots and says that he's healthy, too."

"That's great news," said Alec.

Henry looked toward the barn. "There's a phone in there, right? I have to make a call to the track."

"Yes, in the tack room," Alec said.

"Is there anything I can do?" Danielle asked Alec as Henry walked off.

"You can help me set the wings on the sides of the ramp," Alec said. As the two of them went to work, sharp sounds of hooves striking metal, followed by a shrill scream, could be heard from inside the van.

"Wow! Raven sounds like he wants out *bad,*" said Danielle.

Alec frowned and double-checked the ramp and extensions to make sure they were secure. Then he opened the van doors and stepped through. A loud snort and the sound of furious pawing came from inside the van. *What's up with Raven?* wondered Danielle. *That doesn't sound like him, all noisy and uncomfortable.*

The young stallion sounded as if he was about to go psycho.

CHAPTER THREE

Battle Cry!

"Need a hand?" Danielle called to Alec.

"I think so," he answered. "Henry says that Raven was acting cranky the whole way here. Maybe you'll have better luck with him."

Alec handed Danielle one end of the lead shank. Then he took a step back and gave Raven a slap on the rump. Danielle pulled on the lead as Raven's forefeet touched the ramp. There was a quick rush of hoofbeats as he clattered out of the van. Danielle jumped clear as Raven bolted ahead, nearly mowing her down.

The shank jerked and slithered through Danielle's hands. She desperately clutched the end, but it slipped from her grasp. Alec quickly jumped out of the van and took the shank from her.

"Sorry," Danielle said. "I guess I wasn't ready again."

"That's okay," Alec said, but Danielle could see

he was frowning slightly. He turned Raven in a tight circle and then stopped. The big black colt gave a puzzled snort and twisted his head to face Danielle, his eyes large and fired with excitement.

What a horse, Danielle told herself. *He can be an angel when he wants. But other times...*

Before finishing that thought too harshly, Danielle remembered that she should be grateful for one thing. It was Raven, after all, who had made these past few months endurable without Redman.

Her gaze settled on the colt again. He was such a handsome thing. According to Alec, Raven had inherited the best qualities of both his dam and his sire, the famous Black. Danielle had known him all his young life and watched him develop from a baby to a teenager.

To Henry and Alec he might be Raven, the up-and-coming track star, but to Danielle, he would always be her Little Buddy. There wasn't much little about him anymore, though.

At almost fifteen hands, the colt was tall, and still growing. She could see the fine, hard muscles standing out beneath his sleek coat. Danielle didn't know much about bloodlines. But she *did* know that seeing the graceful black colt galloping around the pasture in the mornings always made her feel good.

Raven pawed the ground, his bright eyes flashing and his ears pricked. "Easy, fella." Alec moved to

Raven's head and tugged gently on the halter. The big colt completely ignored him. Alec whispered soft words into the colt's ear and stepped away. He pulled a little harder on the colt's lead. Raven took a reluctant half step forward.

"Good boy," Alec encouraged him.

Raven finally skittered ahead, dancing briefly at the end of the line. Alec moved closer beside him and took hold of his halter. Suddenly, Raven seemed to rebel, springing back on his haunches and half rearing. Alec moved with him as the colt pulled backward, keeping a firm grip on the colt's halter. "Easy, buddy boy," he soothed.

Danielle trailed behind Alec as he led Raven to the barn and into his stall. The colt threw his head up, his ears seeming to swivel in all directions at once. Danielle held her breath as he began pawing at the stall floor.

Although Alec seemed to be taking Raven's tantrum in stride, Danielle couldn't help but wonder what was provoking all these strange fits. Raven had been such a calm horse the week before. *What did they do to him at South Wind?* she wondered. *What happened?*

"Easy, fella," Alec said softly. "Settle down, now."

Alec must have seen the puzzled look in Danielle's eyes and guessed what she was thinking. "Don't worry, Danielle," he said. "Raven just had a real big dose of the outside world, and it probably made him a little jittery."

"Do you think that's all it is?" she asked anxiously as she gingerly reached out to touch Raven's nose. But the colt moved farther back into his stall.

"He's calming down now," Alec said quietly. "He'll be okay."

Danielle nodded. It must have spooked Raven to be around all those horses for the past few weeks after being alone at the farm. She certainly hoped that the colt wouldn't have a bad reaction to Redman's arrival. So far, however, it didn't seem that Raven had even noticed Reddy.

Taking a carrot from her pocket, Danielle held it out for Raven. The big colt took a step closer, his head extended. But then he suddenly stopped, his nostrils quivering.

"He probably smells Redman on you," Alec said. Danielle began to take her hand away, but Alec shook his head. "Keep it there, Danielle. He'll come over to you. Just be patient."

Sure enough, a few moments later, Raven took the carrot from Danielle's hand and moved to the door. Danielle and Alec both patted him affectionately.

Henry came out of the tack room. "Let's go, Alec," he said briskly as he started out to the van.

Alec turned to Danielle. "Henry has to get over

to Calder. One of our fillies has a race coming up there," he said. "Can I leave Raven in your hands while I drive Henry back to South Wind? I shouldn't be gone long."

"Sure," Danielle said quickly. She was eager for the chance to help out and show Alec that she could be trusted to care for Raven and Redman on her own.

Alec pressed a finger to the side of his chin and thought for a moment. "Hmm, let's see," he said. "I guess all you really have to do is give Raven his lunch and then turn him out."

"Where?"

"Anywhere," Alec answered, "but keep him away from Redman, okay? We should give those two more time to get acquainted before they pasture together. The way Raven is acting right now makes me think we'd better not rush things."

Danielle nodded. "Raven sure does seem wound up, that's for sure."

Alec didn't seem worried. "It's natural for two strange horses to start off by testing each other a bit. Putting them in separate pastures is the best we can do for the time being."

Danielle let Raven sniff her hand before she gave him a pat on the neck, not wanting to startle him. "I'll move Redman to the upper pasture and turn Raven out in the lower. Okay?"

Alec nodded. "Sounds good. I'll be back as soon as we get Henry fixed up. It shouldn't take too long."

After Alec had left, Danielle stepped over to the feed box. She scooped up a crumbly mixture of grains, roughage, and molasses for Raven to eat. It was the same sort of concentrated protein feed given to all Thoroughbreds so that they could build muscle and cut fat from their necks and bodies. A horse like Redman, on the other hand, lived mostly on hay and a little grain.

While Raven ate, Danielle pitched some fresh straw in the stall. Then she returned to the pasture where Redman was reacquainting himself with the sights and smells of the local terrain. Right now, he was happily sampling a patch of flavorful grass. She went over and ran her hand through the paint's long red mane. Then the two of them walked to the gate that separated the upper and lower pastures.

Danielle unlatched the gate and swung it open. Redman's ears pricked up as she nudged him through the opening. The big paint bobbed his head a moment and then took off at a canter, his head held high and his tail flying in the breeze.

Boy, is it good to see him home again, thought Danielle. She tore herself away from watching her horse and returned to the barn to see if Raven had finished his lunch. She heard rustling inside his stall as she walked up the center aisle.

"I guess there's nothing wrong with your appetite," she told the colt as she glanced at his empty feed trough. A moment later, she led him from the barn and through the paddock to the lower pasture.

Keeping up a steady flow of singsong coaxing, she unbuckled and removed Raven's halter. The colt immediately rushed off, tossing his head in a fit of bucking and playing.

Suddenly, Redman's piercing whistle sounded from the direction of the upper pasture. Raven turned his head and froze. Redman called out again.

Is that a welcome? wondered Danielle. *Or is it a challenge?*

As if answering her question, Raven called back. This time, there was no question. It was definitely an unfriendly exchange.

Raven uttered another shrill scream, and his ears swept back flat against his head. Seconds later, he and Redman were galloping madly toward each other. In a few strides, only the wooden fence rails would be keeping them apart!

Danielle's heart froze. A scream choked in her throat.

"No!"

CHAPTER FOUR

Face-off

Shrill whinnies and whistles filled the air. Danielle ran after Raven as fast as she could, calling in vain for him to stop.

But the colt was still heading straight for Redman.

The paint was the first to reach the fence separating the two horses. He pulled up from his charge just before slamming into the wooden rails. Then, he started pacing back and forth, snorting, his ears pricked. *What's the matter with them?* Danielle asked herself. *How could my two favorite horses be threatening each other like this?*

Raven slid to a stop, striking his hoofs against a fence post, nearly shattering the wood.

"Stop it! Stop this right now!" Danielle screamed as loudly as possible. She tried not to think about what would happen if the two horses started fighting. She knew there would be nothing she could do. She was

alone and empty-handed. What was she supposed to do?

Telling herself not to panic, Danielle ran after Redman. She knew that no matter how mad he might be, Redman would never intentionally hurt her. Whether he would listen to her enough to calm down in his present state of mind was another story, though.

She watched as Redman tossed his head and thrashed his tail. Something about his body language told Danielle that the paint was more surprised than angry. Although it was comforting for her to realize that Redman wasn't as mad as she had originally believed, she still thought that her horse's behavior was wrong. He was acting as if he wanted to know what Raven was doing in *his* pasture. But Redman would have to realize that the pasture wasn't just for him any longer. And he'd have to realize that *very soon.*

On the other side of the fence, Raven definitely looked ready to fight. There was nothing playful in the way he arched his neck and stiffened his legs. His body seemed to swell to twice its normal size. He appeared more like a hostile stallion than the flighty young colt that Danielle had been helping to care for these past few months.

Raven stalked along the fence, his eyes large and fixed on Redman. He charged the rails again, lunging and swerving away at the last second.

In response, Redman lashed his tail and flattened his ears back against his head. He raised a foreleg and pawed the ground, as if serving warning.

Raven's gaze remained locked on the paint, and he began moving closer to the fence.

Danielle caught her breath. *Calm down,* she told herself. *Use your head. What would Alec do?*

"That's enough, you two! Stop it right now!" Danielle called. She tried to make her voice as firm and forceful as possible. "Break it up this second!"

But the horses refused to listen. Danielle repeated her orders. "Break it up *right now!*"

This time, Raven seemed to hear her and turned away from the fence. Just as Danielle heaved a heavy sigh of relief, the colt took a few steps back. Then he suddenly lunged toward Redman!

The paint froze, preparing to face off against the brazen young stallion. His muscles looked tense and ready to spring into action.

"Ho!" Danielle called angrily. She quickly pulled off the sweatshirt tied around her waist and waved it in the air. Then she ran over to the fence and bravely put herself between the two horses. She continued waving her arms and shaking her head as she turned to face the colt.

Raven threw his head back and snorted. Hatred flashed in his dark eyes. His muscles bunched up as he rose on his hind legs and pawed the air. Ears flat, he jerked his head defiantly from side to side. He bared his teeth and then began shrilling wildly before bringing his forefeet back to the ground again.

Danielle had never seen a horse act this way before, much less her Raven, her Little Buddy. No matter how bad he was acting, she knew she had to gain control of the situation—and fast. There was no Alec around to come to her aid. It was all up to her.

Using force alone would do no good, Danielle realized. She wasn't strong enough to pull either of the horses away. And even if she could, what if the other horse suddenly charged them? Quickly, she decided that she had only one option. She would have to divert their attention, or the situation would spin completely out of control.

Steeling herself, Danielle slipped through the fence and stepped over to where Redman was holding his ground.

"Easy, boy," she said. Leaning against him, she began to push. Gradually, to her relief, the paint yielded. She managed to turn him so that he was facing away from the colt. Flinging out his hoofs wildly on the other side of the fence, Raven could only watch as Redman showed his back. Then, very slowly, Danielle walked Redman uphill and away from Raven. She needed to put as much distance as possible between the two horses. When they reached the fence at the farthest side of the upper pasture, Danielle removed a few rails to open a gap wide enough for Redman to get out.

After Redman walked through, Danielle replaced the rails. Then she boosted herself up and slid onto Redman's back. She nudged him into a slow walk, and they took to the trail that led into the woods bordering the neighbors' cow pasture.

Redman felt tense beneath her, but he began to relax as they moved away from Raven. Danielle turned to look back at the colt behind them. Raven had moved away from the fence and was watching each step they took. He neighed a few times but was unable to do anything more. Danielle took a deep breath. She had done it, all by herself.

Then she had a terrible thought. What if she was just delaying the inevitable? *No,* she told herself. *I'll make these two friends somehow. They'll have to learn to get along. Otherwise, how can they live in the same barn together?*

The sandy path that Redman was following led into a forest of oak and pine. Now it was Danielle's turn to relax on the familiar trail. She always tried to anticipate what was coming around the bend, even if she already knew it by heart. It had always been kind of a game for her and Reddy.

The trail led into a large field, where Danielle

urged Redman into a slow trot, then a gallop. Danielle knew it was risky to be riding bareback, especially after the scene with Raven. Besides, she had already been dumped once this morning. But somehow it felt so natural that she couldn't resist.

Redman moved sweetly and obediently under her hands, like a delicate, well-oiled machine. Wind whistled past Danielle's ears, taking her worries with it. She breathed in the smell of grass and her horse's sweat and felt the warmth of the sun. Redman seemed happier, too. He shifted gaits beneath her, slowing down almost effortlessly.

They came to the end of the stretch that banked into a wide, arching turn, and Redman cantered gently to a walk. Danielle reached forward and gave the big paint a warm slap on the neck as he drew to a stop. Danielle slid off Redman's back, feeling as if she'd just woken up from a beautiful dream. When she gave Reddy another pat, the paint started flinging his head up, playfully tousling his forelock. "Such a good boy," she told him.

Walking side by side, they soon reached the top of the hill above the upper pasture. They stopped and gazed down at the farm. The white rails around the pastures and paddocks flashed in the sunlight. The sight was so beautiful that Danielle gave a contented sigh. There was definitely no place like home.

After a few moments, Danielle shifted her attention back to the problem at hand. *We'll have to return to the farm soon, and then Redman and Raven will face off again,* she thought. As long as both horses were going to be stabled together, another confrontation was almost unavoidable.

A shiver ran through her at the thought of having to repeat that scene. She'd known, of course, that some friction between Redman and Raven was possible, and Alec had warned her, but she had never expected anything like this.

Danielle looked past the paddock and the barn and was relieved to see Alec's truck in the driveway. *He'll know what to do about these two,* she thought. At least now she wouldn't have to handle the situation on her own.

Danielle turned to look Redman in the eyes. "Ready to give it another try, big guy?"

Redman harrumphed.

With her hand on his neck, Danielle led Redman through the gap in the upper pasture fence. They had hardly reached the middle of the field before Raven started shrilling a new challenge.

Danielle took a deep breath. It was beginning already!

Redman pricked up his ears and snorted, but he walked calmly beside Danielle. When it was clear that Raven wouldn't stop carrying on, Danielle turned Redman around. "Be still," she told him. *Please,* she added silently. The paint quietly dropped his head and whiffed the grass around his forefeet.

Alec came out of the barn to see what was causing all the commotion. He looked out into the pasture and waved to Danielle. Danielle gestured to Raven and then Redman. Then she held her hands palms-up and shook her head.

Alec seemed to understand and waved for her to keep Redman back. He quickly stepped inside the barn and returned a few moments later with a halter and lead shank. Running out to the lower pasture, he called the colt. Raven ignored him. The colt's attention was focused on Redman.

After a few attempts, Alec was able to get the halter securely over Raven's head. Clipping on the lead shank, he quietly turned the colt around a few times and then led him back to the barn. Dizzy, Raven squealed and snorted most of the way back. Danielle shook her head. That colt was a handful, all right.

After Alec had locked Raven in his stall, Danielle walked Redman slowly into the lower pasture. The big paint went trotting off, his head held high. When Alec finally walked over to Danielle, she told him about the face-off.

"I guess we should have left him in his stall," Alec said, frowning.

"Raven's acting like this is his own private little

kingdom," Danielle told him. "He's treating poor Reddy like an invader." Then, feeling she was being unfair, she added, "At first, Reddy did the same thing. But then he seemed to calm down."

Alec nodded. "I'll move Raven down to the stall at the far end of the barn. That'll put some distance between them. Maybe it will help for the time being."

"But this fighting won't go on forever, right?" asked Danielle. "How long do you figure Raven—I mean *they* will keep this up?"

"Raven's just showing off for Redman," Alec said, shrugging. "He's testing him, that's all. But there's no harm in it, Danielle. Raven's a good boy. You know that, right?"

Danielle nodded slowly. "Was he acting like this over at South Wind?"

Alec shook his head. "No way. If anything, he seemed a little nervous and shy. But that's because he hadn't been living there for three months already."

That makes sense, thought Danielle. *South Wind must have seemed pretty strange to Raven after having the farm all to himself.*

"I think some of the older horses probably intimidated him a little, too," Alec said.

Danielle glanced over at the barn, where the colt had started neighing again. Now Raven's bizarre behavior was beginning to make sense. "So when he came back here expecting to have the farm all to himself..."

Alec nodded. "That's right. This is his home and his territory. I guess he wants Redman to know that, too."

"I think everyone for miles around must know that now. Little Buddy can make a lot of noise when he wants to!"

Alec laughed. "He'll settle down soon enough. Don't you worry. We just have to be patient."

Danielle walked over to Redman and stroked the big paint's nose. *Alec sure does know what he's talking about,* she thought. But she couldn't help feeling that the conflict between her two favorite horses had only just begun.

CHAPTER FIVE

Dad

Raven began to settle down over the next few days, just as Alec had predicted. His aggressive posturing stopped. He no longer snorted and carried on whenever he came close to Redman. The two horses weren't quite sharing the same feed bucket yet, but at least they were respecting each other's boundaries.

Danielle still didn't understand why her two favorite horses couldn't get along. The situation made her feel sort of helpless. She had to play favorites practically every time she walked into the barn.

Raven was kept busy with his training schedule, while Redman readjusted to the easy life at the Conners farm. Except for his rides with Danielle, Reddy spent most of his time idly grazing in the upper pasture. His curiosity about Raven had now turned into complete lack of interest. He just ignored the colt whenever he saw him. And this seemed to drive Raven nuts. It seemed the colt wanted any kind of reaction from Redman rather than no reaction at all.

Unfortunately for Danielle, she was still caught directly in the middle. Reddy was home for only eleven more days, and she wanted to make the most of their time together. But Raven needed her, too. Alec had her grooming the colt half a dozen times a day, and she was putting in nearly as many sessions with the lead line, walking Raven around the pasture. Running back and forth between the two horses was becoming a full-time job.

After spending most of Monday morning with Raven, Danielle went riding with her best pal, Julie Burke. The two of them took Redman and Calamity, Julie's frisky gray Arabian mare, on a tour of their favorite neighborhood spots. They made it all the way out to the river and even as far as a place they called "The Little World," some undeveloped land on the far side of Wishing Wells.

On the way back, the girls stopped at Table Rock, a resting spot on the low ridge overlooking the Conners farm. They turned their horses loose and flopped to the ground. After a while, Danielle jumped up, headed over to the fence, and climbed up on the top rail. She started walking along the rail like a tightrope walker, then jumped to the ground when she lost her balance. Julie sat up and laughed. "Fancy footwork, hot stuff," she quipped.

"You try it," Danielle challenged her friend.

Julie brushed her hand through her hair, picking at a few blades of grass lodged in her short, dark curls. "No thanks," she said. "A broken leg is the last thing I need right now. Besides, I haven't ridden this far in ages."

Danielle smiled. "I could keep riding forever, I think."

"You're just excited about having Reddy home again," Julie said. "Wait until tonight. You'll feel it then." She glanced downhill to the farm. "Hey, look. Is that a school bus turning in to your driveway?"

Danielle immediately recognized the converted bus pulling off the county road. It was the tour bus for her dad's band! Mr. Conners had called the night before, saying he was trying to make it home for a few days. But they hadn't expected him home until tomorrow.

"It's my dad!" Danielle said excitedly to Julie.

"*That's* the bus your dad's band travels in?" Julie asked doubtfully.

Danielle nodded. "Sometimes. They've been going all over the country since that "Sky Riders" song of Dad's made the charts."

"That must be cool, playing music and getting paid for it."

Danielle shrugged. "Dad says it can be pretty tough on the road. We need the money, though, so he says he's going to keep touring as long as he can."

Julie nodded sympathetically. "It must be hard for you guys to be apart so much."

Danielle was getting anxious to see her dad. "Want to come down to the house?"

"Thanks, but I have to get home myself," Julie said, getting to her feet and heading toward Calamity. "See ya."

Danielle immediately sprinted over to where Redman was grazing and did a flying belly flop into his saddle, scrambling into the seat. Then she raced toward the bus, galloping as fast as Redman could take her. After quickly pulling off the saddle and tack, Danielle left Reddy in the paddock and ran to meet her dad.

"Hey!" she called as the bus lumbered to a stop. The doors opened and Jack Tagger and Clyde Katz got out. Jack and Clyde were backup musicians in the band. Danielle had known them for ages and thought they were two of the nicest adults she'd ever met. Clyde was stocky and wore heavy, black-framed glasses on his round face. Jack was beanpole slim with a long face. Behind them came Danielle's father. With his freckled cheeks and reddish blond hair, he looked like a grown-up version of her brother, Dylan. He was a handsome man in a rough sort of way.

Kyle Conners held his arms open wide as Danielle ran toward him. He swept her off her feet in a big bear hug. "Who is this beautiful young lady?"

"Cut it out, Dad!"

"Where's your mother, honey? I want to surprise her, too."

"Her car's gone," Danielle said, glancing over at the house. "I think she's at work."

A frown clouded the big man's face.

"It might be some rush project they're doing," Danielle said quickly.

"And Dylan?" Mr. Conners asked.

Danielle shrugged. "He's probably hanging around somewhere."

Mr. Conners turned to Jack and Clyde. Danielle noticed that the three men looked tired, as if they had been on the road for a long time and hadn't slept much. They all wore collared shirts, jeans, and sneakers. "Go on inside and see if there's anything to drink in the fridge, boys. I have to visit with my daughter here a minute."

"Sure thing," Clyde said, grinning. "Introduce her to the latest member of the band." He and Jack nudged each other as if sharing some inside joke and then walked toward the house.

Danielle was confused. A new band member? Just then, she heard an odd sound coming from inside the bus.

Bwawk bwawk. Buck kawp. Then came a sort of fluttering noise, like a bird flapping its wings. Except these were some *loud* fluttering sounds, Danielle told herself. The kind only a *huge* bird would make.

Danielle looked at her dad. His sky-blue eyes were sparkling.

Bwawk bwawk, buck kawp, buck buck buh kawp.

"What *is* that?" Danielle asked. Her dad motioned for her to follow him into the bus.

As they edged their way past seats, guitar cases, amplifiers, a table, and a portable refrigerator, the sounds grew even louder. Danielle and her dad stopped way in the back beside what looked like an amplifier with a blanket tossed over it.

"Okay, I give up. What is it, Dad?"

"This old guy was driving us crazy before we found this blanket. Once we threw it over him, he slept for most of the ride. Sure sounds awake now, doesn't he?"

When Mr. Conners removed the blanket, Danielle's mouth dropped open. "A chicken?" she said.

"A rooster, honey." Her dad smiled mischievously. "And not just any rooster. This is Dooley, a member of the famous cabaret act The Leslie Loon

Duo. We were touring with Madam Leslie and Dooley on a double bill up in Memphis a while back. Leslie is an old pal of ours. And guess what? Dooley here can play the piano. Well, it's actually a toy piano," he added when Danielle looked skeptical.

"Unfortunately, Madam Leslie was in a car accident the other day," Mr. Conners went on. "She's all right, but she's going to be laid up for a bit, so I offered to bring Dooley to the farm until she can come get him."

Dooley crowed loudly. *Er-er-er-rooh. Er-er-er-rooh.*

"Great," Danielle said doubtfully.

"Quite a pair of lungs on the old boy. But he's one heck of a piano player. Not a bad dancer, either."

Dooley started rustling around, scratching and flapping his wings. Danielle noticed that one wing was taped to his side.

"What happened there?" she asked her dad.

"He got into a scrape with some bartender's dog up in Macon."

"Really?" Danielle asked. "Poor guy."

"Yep." Danielle's dad shook his head. "It's been quite a week for Dooley here."

"But you should have seen what he did to the dog," called Clyde, stepping into the front of the bus.

"Yes, sir-ree!" cheered Jack, who was following

behind him. Both men were loaded down with cans of soda and pieces of cold fried chicken.

"That is the fightingest old rooster I've ever seen," Clyde said, sitting down at the table.

"Better not get too close with that chicken leg, Jack," Mr. Conners warned. "Ol' Dooley might think you have plans for him, too."

Jack looked at the chicken leg in his hand and made a face. "Now why'd you have to go and say that? You've darn near ruined my appetite. Makes me feel terrible."

Clyde chuckled. "You feel bad for a chicken, Jack?"

"Hey, it's just that Dooley and I've been gettin' to know each other pretty well the past couple of days," answered Jack. "And I almost hate to think I might be eating one of his girlfriends."

Clyde grabbed the chicken leg out of Jack's hand. "Well, if you don't want it..."

Jack snatched the drumstick back. "I said *almost.*"

CHAPTER SIX

Dooley

Dooley continued to flutter around inside the big wire cage in the back of the bus. Every now and then, he threw his head back and crowed loudly.

"I thought roosters only did that at sunup," Danielle complained, covering her ears.

"Well, with ol' Dooley here, it's whenever he darn well feels like it." Mr. Conners looked into the cage. "What do you say, Dooley, fella? Ready to see your new quarters?"

"Alec is going to love this," said Danielle, chuckling. "He's just gotten used to Dylan's ferrets, and now he's going to have to put up with a chicken."

"Rooster," corrected Mr. Conners. "Where is Ramsay, anyway?"

"Well, his truck's here, so I guess he's in the barn with Raven. They've been doing a lot of stall work lately. Or he could always be in the Coop," she added, pointing to the small house where Alec

Ramsay had been living the past few months. It had been converted from an old chicken coop.

Danielle's dad nodded to Jack and Clyde. "Come on, guys," he said. "Let's move Mister Big Foot out to the barn."

Jack and Clyde each took a side of Dooley's cage and carried the rooster from the bus. Dooley sat quietly, gazing out through the wire mesh. Danielle thought he looked like a prince observing the countryside as his bearers carried him along the way.

The men placed Dooley's cage in an empty corner in the hay shed. Danielle was immediately impressed at the rooster's calmness in his new surroundings.

"This little shed isn't much more than four posts and an aluminum roof, but at least it's a dry place for him when it rains," said Mr. Conners.

Dooley hopped out once Danielle's dad opened the cage door. Twisting his head in various directions, he strutted around, inspecting the area. *Bwawk bwawk, buck kawp, buck buck buh kawp.* Danielle had to stifle a giggle.

"We can fence off an area to make a pen for him here," said Mr. Conners. "There's still a roll of chicken wire in the garage, right, Danielle?"

Danielle nodded, still watching Dooley. As her dad and his friends headed to the garage, Danielle and the rooster were left in the shed alone. Dooley came closer to Danielle. "Nice bird," she said, reaching out to stroke his neck. As she did, Dooley pecked at her hand in a friendly sort of way. "Ow," Danielle said, quickly pulling back. The rooster suddenly popped into the air, flapping his good wing. He kept up the one-wing flap all the way out into the driveway.

"Hey!" called Danielle. "Come here, you crazy bird!" She started to chase after him, but then finally gave up. *Might as well give him a chance to take a look around,* she told herself.

As Danielle watched Dooley snooping about, she couldn't help but be surprised at how handsome he was. She would never have thought of calling a rooster a pretty animal. Although she lived on a farm, she'd rarely seen any live chickens up close. Her family had stopped raising poultry before she was born. That didn't really bother Danielle much. *Horses are all I need,* she told herself.

But something about Dooley intrigued Danielle. His feathers were brown, orange, and yellow, with gleaming tail feathers that were long and curvy and shone greenish black in the sunlight. From his tall red comb to his big dinosaur feet, Dooley seemed to know that he was one good-looking bird. *Must be because he's in show business,* Danielle decided.

The tape on Dooley's bad wing had come loose and it flopped at his side like a half-opened fan. It didn't seem to bother the rooster, though. Eyeing Danielle, he confidently pulled himself up to his full height and stretched his good wing.

Mr. Conners and his friends returned with the roll of chicken wire and set to work to transform the little shed into a temporary pen. Just as they were finishing up, Alec Ramsay came into the shed.

"A rooster, huh?" he said, raising his eyebrows.

Mr. Conners filled Alec in on the Dooley situation as the bird squawked a tune to himself in the backyard.

"So he won't be here too long," said Mr. Conners finished. "Just a few days is all."

"No problem," said Alec. "It'll make things more interesting around the farm, I'm sure." He winked at Danielle. Danielle grinned back.

Mr. Conners glanced over at the barn. "So how's the colt making out?"

"Oh, he has his moments," Alec said. "And sometimes he doesn't. Almost every horse ever foaled has some kind of hang-up, I guess. But this guy will eventually be worth the trouble it's taking to set him straight."

"So how long before we see Raven at the track?" asked Danielle's dad. "Are you going to race him as a two-year-old?"

"Too early to tell," Alec answered. "He hasn't even officially started training yet."

The men chatted a few minutes longer until Alec announced he had to get back to South Wind. Mr. Conners kissed Danielle on the cheek and then headed to town to drop off Jack and Clyde. That left Danielle alone again, except for the horses...and Dooley.

As Danielle headed toward the paddock, Redman hung his head over the fence to watch her approach. She slipped through the fence, and the paint nudged her shoulder with his nose, then started sniffing her pockets.

"Hey, what do you think I am, your personal carrot tree?" Danielle teased. Redman nudged her shoulder a bit more in an attempt to convince Danielle that it was playtime.

Danielle smiled. "You're such a big kid, you know that?" Redman continued nudging her shoulder. Danielle pushed back.

"You always want to play, huh, boy? Well, I hate to let you down, but there's work to be done first," Danielle told him. "I have to check one of the fence rails on the far side of the paddock."

Redman tagged along behind her, kicking up his hooves and flashing his tail from side to side. The big paint wasn't about to give up on playtime.

Danielle frowned as she jiggled the loose fence rail around, trying to fit it tightly into the post. Redman leaned over her shoulder as if he was spying. "Okay, big guy," said Danielle, "how about some food now? Will that make you happy?" Redman tossed his head.

"You know, I almost forgot what a stubborn horse you can be," she told him as they walked together to the barn. "You sure are something." Once she led Redman to his stall, he immediately started munching hay. Scooping up a container full of oats from the feed bin, Danielle took Redman the rest of his dinner.

Raven stood on the other end of the barn. He had been acting sullen since the day before and was barely making a sound now. Danielle left Redman and walked down the aisle to see the unhappy colt.

"Hey, Little Buddy," she called through the screened-in upper door.

Raven ignored her and sniffed at something in the corner of his stall. For a moment he turned halfway toward her, enabling Danielle to see the splash of white on his forehead.

Danielle undid the stall door latch and stepped inside. The colt lifted his head, moved back, and glared at her as she moved beside him.

"Come on, Raven. Don't be spiteful now. You're still my Little Buddy." She found a soft brush and rub rag and gave him a quick going-over.

Alec always told her that Raven needed as much daily handling as she could give him. He especially needed it around the feet. Usually, the colt loved these light grooming sessions. Today, however, it seemed he could barely tolerate Danielle in his stall. He snorted and even lashed out with a hind hoof.

Danielle jumped back. Then, from the other end of the barn, she heard Redman whinny. Raven cringed slightly, swishing his tail several times like a whip.

Oh, boy, thought Danielle. *Here we go again.*

She'd been hoping that the trouble between the two horses was just a short adjustment phase they were both going through. But neither of them seemed to have any intention of changing his ways.

What if it was permanent?

CHAPTER SEVEN

Raven's Time

Danielle hadn't talked with Julie Burke since they last went riding together. So when Julie rode her bike by the farm a few days before Christmas, Danielle was excited to see her friend.

"Hey, Julie!" Danielle called from the barn door, waving.

"Hi," said Julie, hopping off her bike. "How's everything going?"

"Oh, not so bad. The usual, I guess."

"My cousins from up north are visiting for the holidays," Julie said.

"Yeah? Are you guys having fun?"

Julie just shrugged.

"That much, huh?" said Danielle, laughing. She'd met Julie's little cousins before.

The two of them walked down the barn aisle to Raven's stall. Alec was there, working on the colt.

"I've been helping Alec with this guy a lot," Danielle told Julie as she peered into Raven's stall.

Alec was gently rubbing a saddle pad over Raven's back and shoulders and talking to the black colt, chanting in a soft voice. He was trying to make the colt feel at ease with the foreign object touching his back. In just a few months, Alec had told Danielle, many different jockeys would be sitting on the colt's back. They needed to get Raven used to that idea.

"Lay, lay, lay, ahhhh..." Alec crooned. "La-la-la, ahhh. Lay, lay, lay."

Julie looked at Danielle questioningly, but Danielle put a finger to her lips. Even though she knew what Alec was *doing*, she had no idea what he was *saying*. The tone of Alec's voice seemed to be all that the colt cared about, though. It was a very soothing tone, something that a mother might use to coax her baby to sleep.

Alec continued to calm Raven for a while. When he finally glanced up at Danielle, she stepped to the stall half door. He handed her the saddle pad. "Okay, Danielle. I guess it's about that time."

Danielle nodded and headed over to the tack room. She hung up the saddle pad and came back with a light bridle. Alec turned Raven around a few times. The colt didn't seem to enjoy that very much. He thrashed his tail and whinnied very loudly. Alec tried to soothe him by running his hands over the colt's shoulders and down to his knees.

After a while, Alec stood up and stepped back. Then he signaled Danielle to hand him the bridle. Alec cooed to Raven as he slipped the bridle on and eased the rubber bit into the colt's mouth.

Raven played with the bit briefly. Then he suddenly began to act up again, baring his teeth and huffing and puffing. Alec spoke to the colt gently as he petted him affectionately. A few moments later, Raven settled down.

Danielle pulled Julie away from the stall door, leaving Alec alone with Raven. The colt whinnied softly but managed to stay still. The girls walked quietly to the other end of the barn.

"Now I believe you when you said Raven's been acting cranky these days," Julie said. "Wow."

"He's a lot better now," said Danielle. "It was pretty noisy in here a few days ago, with Redman just getting here and Alec starting in with the bridle and all. Raven still gets wild sometimes, but he's being pretty good today." *So far,* she added silently.

"My dad says you have to be patient," said Julie. Her dad had been training yearlings for a long time, so Danielle always trusted her friend's opinions when it came to horses.

"Alec's patient, all right," Danielle said. "And he's *very* organized. He always does everything in order. We do everything for Raven at the same time of day so it becomes a routine."

Julie nodded in agreement. "What about Redman?" she asked. "Are those two still snarling at each other? Or have they worked things out?"

"Not exactly," sighed Danielle. "But as long as they have their own private areas to run around in, there isn't too much trouble between them. Reddy's alone in the upper pasture now."

"I know. I saw the poor guy on the way in," Julie said.

"Do you mind going to the house a second?" said Danielle, changing the subject. "I want to see if my dad's awake yet."

"No problem," said Julie, shrugging.

"Hey, Alec, do you need any help right now?" Danielle asked Alec.

"No," he replied, giving the colt another reassuring pat. "Everything's under control. You girls go on and have some fun."

It was quiet inside the Conners house as the girls walked through the front door. Danielle could hear light snoring coming from her parents' room.

"Dad's still asleep," she told Julie. They went into the kitchen, and Danielle poured two glasses of iced tea from the refrigerator.

"Why's your dad sleeping at this time of day?" Julie whispered. "Is he sick or something?"

"No," Danielle replied, slicing up some lemon. "His band played late last night. He didn't get home till this morning. He was just coming in when I was getting up."

"Wow," whispered Julie. "That's pretty late, all right."

"At least he'll be home a few more days before the band gets back on the road," Danielle said. "We're lucky these Florida gigs came up at the last minute. If they hadn't, he might not have been home for Christmas."

Danielle motioned to the door, and the girls moved outside to the porch steps to enjoy their cool iced tea.

Er-uhr-uhr-roo. Er-uhr-uhr-roo, came a familiar sound from the direction of the hay shed.

Julie looked at Danielle in surprise. "Since when do you guys have chickens?"

Danielle chuckled. "I guess I didn't tell you about Dooley."

Julie shook her head.

"Well, he's actually a rooster with a broken wing who plays the piano," Danielle told her friend.

"He plays the *piano*?"

Danielle shrugged. "A toy piano, from what my dad says. I haven't actually witnessed it. Want to check him out?"

Dooley was strutting about when the girls

reached his pen on the other side of barn. He welcomed them with another *cock-a-doodle-do.* Raven whinnied in response from inside the barn. Out in the pasture, Redman kept grazing.

"Check out those green tail feathers," Danielle said, pointing.

"That's so cool," Julie said. "Maybe we should dye our hair that color!"

Danielle laughed. "I don't think my mom would be too thrilled about that." She called to the rooster, who was doing a little dance now. It looked as if he wanted her to throw a handful of feed.

"Hey, he dances, too," said Julie as the rooster scratched stylishly around in the dirt. "That's pretty amazing."

"Danielle! Can you give me a hand here?" Alec called from inside the barn.

"I guess it's time to go back to work," said Danielle, a little reluctantly.

Julie stayed with Dooley as Danielle climbed over the paddock fence and ran to the barn. She came out a few minutes later, carrying a soccer ball. Raven was high-stepping behind her on the lead line, blinking in the bright sunshine.

Danielle and the black colt took a quick tour of the paddock. Raven bounced around, acting frisky. Julie ran over to the fence to watch.

"Hey, Jule, come on," Danielle called to her

friend. "Want to go for a run with me and Raven? It's time for him to get some exercise."

"Sure!" said Julie, eagerly hopping over the fence. Together, the girls led the colt through the gate into the lower pasture.

Off at the far end of the upper pasture, Redman looked up from his grazing and whinnied. Raven pricked up his ears and whinnied back. Though the exchange didn't seem particularly threatening, it didn't sound very friendly, either. "Be good, both of you," Danielle ordered sharply.

She took off Raven's halter and lead line. Then she and Julie kicked the ball back and forth between them. Hopefully, Danielle thought, Raven would become interested in something besides Redman on the other side of the fence.

The big paint slowly wound his way toward them. He stopped midfield, watching Danielle and Julie trying to distract the black colt.

Danielle glanced over her shoulder at Redman. He was doing a little dance, almost like Dooley, to let her know that he wanted to play, too. *But this is Raven's time,* she told herself. She had promised not to let Redman's time at the farm interfere with her work with the colt. But seeing Redman acting like that broke her heart just the same. She had only a week left until she had to return him to North Carolina. *And how am I even going to* get *him north?*

Danielle suddenly wondered. Too bad Julie's pesky northern cousins weren't horse people, with a handy van. Danielle sighed. She'd been pushing this whole problem to the back of her mind for days.

Now Raven was chasing Julie and the soccer ball across the pasture. Danielle gave one last look back at Redman before returning her full attention to the colt.

I still love you, Reddy. Please don't be mad at me.

CHAPTER EIGHT

Jealous

Raven pranced about with springy steps as he watched Julie dribble the soccer ball along the fence. When Julie kicked the ball to Danielle, he tossed his head and, snorting, began to chase after it. He ran toward Danielle and swooped by her, just like the big black bird he was named for.

When the colt finally came to a stop, Danielle stroked him affectionately. Redman whinnied from the other side of the fence.

"How's Reddy been doing?" Julie asked Danielle. "Are you getting to spend much time with him?"

"Not as much as I'd like," Danielle admitted. "But it's really nice to have him home again."

"Alec is still paying you to help out with Raven, isn't he?" asked Julie.

"He sure is," Danielle replied. "And it's a good thing, too. I need the money big-time."

"Have you gotten any baby-sitting jobs?" Julie asked sympathetically. She knew that Danielle was saving every penny to bring Redman home for good.

Danielle shook her head. "I'm too busy running back and forth between these two. And with both my dad and Redman here for just a little while..." Danielle sighed. "I sure could use some extra money, though."

Julie nodded. "If I hear of something, I'll let you know."

Danielle shrugged. "I probably wouldn't be able to take any jobs for the next week or so, but thanks anyway."

Raven began to run up and down the field, kicking up his heels and enjoying the sunshine. He dashed by Danielle again, coming within inches of her.

"Hey! Watch it!" Danielle shouted as Raven dodged past her, a little too close for comfort. The colt zoomed by like a train off the tracks. His loud breathing and the drumming of his hooves filled the air.

Danielle and Julie kicked the ball between them a bit more. Raven chased after it like a big, gangly puppy.

After a few more passes, Danielle coaxed the colt to slow to a walk by showing him a carrot. Sweat glistened on Raven's coat as Danielle slipped the halter over his head.

"Okay, Little Buddy," she said. "Recess is over. Time to go back to school." She clipped on the lead line and began walking the colt in circles.

Though Raven had been halter-broken for months, even before leaving his mama, Danielle and Alec had kept up these lessons with the lead line almost every day. Danielle knew the reason for this was to get Raven to *lead,* not just follow her. Alec always said that it could make a big difference later on.

Julie stood outside the circle watching Danielle work the colt at a slow trot. Danielle eased the colt back to a walk and then finally to a stop.

"I have to get going," Julie said. "Give me a call later, okay?"

Raven had begun to snort and dance around now, so Danielle had her hands full. She didn't even try talking Julie into hanging out any longer. "I will. See ya," she called and waved good-bye to her friend.

Fully focusing on Raven, Danielle switched the lead from the left to the right side of the halter to work the colt from the other side. Out of the corner of her eye, she could see Redman watching from the upper pasture, looking lonely. She sighed, knowing that she had to finish her work with Raven, and turned her attention back to the colt. But no matter how hard she tried to avoid it, her thoughts kept returning to Redman.

Letting a bit more line slide through her grip, she clucked to the colt. He responded willingly and widened his circle around her.

"Good boy," she called to Raven. "How come you're so good with me and such a troublemaker around Reddy? Huh, Little Buddy? What's up with that?"

She watched the black colt as he made lazy clockwise circles around her. He seemed to be behaving himself now, his eyes all big and innocent. But Danielle wasn't fooled. She knew that he could be good one minute and bad the next, depending on his mood. Raven was beautiful and smart, but he could also be a handful when he wanted to.

After a few more turns, Danielle eased the colt to a walk again. "That's a good boy," she called.

Raven shook his head as Danielle moved closer to him. He lowered his neck and nibbled at the belt loops of her jeans. Then he nuzzled her chest. He felt warm to Danielle. She pressed her face against his shoulder and breathed in the warm, wet aroma of sweaty horse. Raven dropped his head and chomped a mouthful of grass, then swished at a fly with his tail. "That's my Little Buddy..." Danielle began to croon.

Suddenly, from the upper pasture came the sound of Redman's plaintive whinny. Danielle glanced back helplessly at her old horse.

Raven snorted and stepped away from her, flinging his head from side to side. "Oh stop it, you," Danielle said. "Reddy's only going to be here for a little while. Can't you be nice?" Raven continued to glare in the direction of the paint.

"You have to understand that Reddy's special to me," Danielle tried to explain to the colt. "This is his home, too. It was his way before you came here. Can't you respect that?"

Raven called back to the paint with a shrill cry. They challenged back and forth, Raven puffing up and jerking his lead.

"Stop it now!" Danielle scolded. "You guys have to learn to live together!"

Raven suddenly turned his head. Danielle followed the colt's gaze and saw Redman running along the fence. Raven jerked on the lead, wanting to chase after him. Danielle jerked back.

"No way, mister," she said, shaking her head firmly. "Not a chance."

Raven snorted as if laughing at her.

"Okay then, we'll just have to go inside for a while," said Danielle. "If you don't want to play nice, you won't play at all."

To Danielle's surprise, Raven offered only token

resistance as she pulled on the lead. Moments later, he was walking quietly along beside her. But Danielle figured that Raven wasn't just being obedient. She had a feeling it was more like he was proud of something, as if he had won a game. Redman whinnied and watched them go. The paint was plainly jealous.

Danielle had thought that Raven and Reddy were fighting about territory and establishing their own space. But now she wasn't so sure.

As Danielle led Raven back into the paddock, she realized that the only time Redman paid any attention to the colt was when she was near him.

Reddy doesn't want to share me with another horse, Danielle thought.

And from the way the colt was acting, it seemed that Raven knew Redman didn't want him anywhere near Danielle. But that didn't appear to stop the colt one bit.

It looked as if Raven was actually *trying* to make Reddy jealous.

CHAPTER NINE

Dooley Unleashed

Danielle gave Raven a quick grooming and then left him in his stall to munch hay. As she walked outside, she noticed a blister on the palm of her hand. Her hands had been getting roughened up lately from working with the colt on the lead line. Her arms and shoulders were getting stronger, too.

Danielle started out to the pastures. Redman looked as if he was dozing by the far corner of the upper fence. "Hey, Reddy," she called.

There was no response.

"Reddy!" she called again, and then whistled. But now the big paint seemed more interested in something in the woods than in turning to see her. A few minutes ago, when she'd been with Raven, Redman had whinnied and carried on as if getting her attention was the most important thing in the world. But now he didn't seem to care about her being there at all. Danielle felt a pang of sadness.

She walked through the lower pasture, climbed over the fence, and stopped halfway through the upper pasture, calling to her horse once again. Redman looked up briefly, his ears expressing only a mild curiosity.

"Reddy," Danielle called loudly, waving him toward her. But the paint still wouldn't budge. Danielle stood in the pasture, glaring at her horse. Redman turned his head to face off into the distance. Then, he turned back to Danielle and beckoned with his head for her to come to him.

"Oh, all right, Reddy," Danielle said, laughing. "I guess I can come to you for once."

But to her surprise, when she reached Redman, he barely paid any attention to her at all. He allowed her to pet his coat for a moment, then turned away again. All of his concentration seemed focused on something beyond the fence in the woods. Danielle leaned against the big paint and sighed.

As a soft wind blew over them, Redman intently sniffed the air for scents carried by the breeze. "What is it, Reddy? Is something out there?" Danielle asked. Redman flicked an ear but remained still.

There's nothing out there, Danielle thought. *He's just ignoring me.*

Danielle stepped up on one of the fence rails and boosted herself onto Redman's back. She tried turning him back to the barn, but he just kept walking, in a circle, until he faced the same way again.

Danielle leaned forward onto her horse's neck. "Come on, Reddy. Don't be like this," she whispered in his ear. "Let's go home now, okay?"

With a little more urging, the big paint finally turned back and followed the trail toward the lower pasture and the paddock.

Once in the barn, Raven and Reddy started grumbling at each other, neighing and snorting. Danielle threw up her hands. "Stop that, Reddy! Both of you stop it! Can't you guys just quit fighting?"

Danielle began to groom Redman, running a brush over his coat. "What's the deal, Reddy? I thought you and Raven would start getting along by now. Why are you two doing this to me?"

Redman swished his tail and flicked an ear in her direction as she spoke.

"Danielle," called Mr. Conners from outside the barn. "Where are you, honey?"

"In here, Dad," she called. Mr. Conners walked into the barn and gave Danielle a big hug. Danielle went back to brushing out Redman's mane.

Mr. Conners looked over at Raven's stall. "These two still at it?"

Danielle nodded. "Yep."

Danielle's dad watched as she put Redman in his stall. "So what does Alec have to say about all of this?"

"He says it's good for Raven to have Reddy here because he has to learn to share."

Mr. Conners glanced toward Raven's end of the barn. "I reckon that colt thinks he's the only horse in the world."

Danielle brushed off her jeans as she shut the stall door behind Redman. "You can say that again."

She felt a little guilty about having cut Raven's playtime short earlier in the day, so she walked down to the colt's stall. "Okay, Little Buddy," she said through the door. "It's recess time again. Just promise me that you'll act nice like I know you can."

Leading Raven into the paddock, she slipped off his halter and turned him loose in the lower pasture. Then she climbed over the paddock fence to rejoin her father. Mr. Conners was watching Dooley flap around inside his pen.

The wooden splint on the rooster's injured wing was hanging by a piece of tape. It dragged behind him in the dirt as he skittered about. "I've fixed that darned thing three times already," Mr. Conners said. "It never stays in place for long."

Danielle glanced at her dad. Sunlight glinted off the tiny diamond stud earring in his ear. He'd had it for as long as she could remember, so she couldn't picture him without it.

He stepped inside the chicken-wire pen to fix the dragging splint again. However, Dooley apparently didn't feel like being handled. He kept running around the pen as fast as he could, with Danielle's dad chasing after him. Finally, Mr. Conners grabbed the rooster, barely managing to get the tape loose and the splint off before the ungrateful bird pecked him to death.

"Darned rooster. I have half a mind to..." Mr. Conners muttered. But when he looked at Dooley's wing more closely, he seemed pleasantly surprised. "I'm going to leave this thing off. It looks like his wing has healed up pretty well," he said.

Dooley started hopping around, testing his untaped wing. He skipped out of his pen and up onto the pasture fence rail. Next, he was exploring the barn, flapping from place to place. He finally settled on top of Redman's stall door.

"Hey, get down from there," Danielle called as she and her dad followed the rooster inside the barn.

Mr. Conners laughed. "It's all right, Danielle," he said. "You see? Reddy doesn't seem to mind him."

Redman was watching Dooley from just inside his stall door. He calmly bobbed his head as the rooster edged along the half door and looked around.

"Making yourself right at home, aren't you, Dooley?" Mr. Conners said. "You'd better watch that bird, Danielle. He tends to steal things. He was after my earring for a while there." Danielle's dad grinned.

"Between him and Dylan's ferrets, we're lucky to keep anything around here," Danielle said.

"Shall we put him back in his pen?" Mr. Conners asked.

"That's all right, Dad," Danielle said. "I'll put him back later. I'm staying here in the barn a while longer, anyway."

Mr. Conners gave her a kiss on the cheek. "All right, Danny. I'm going to take care of some business before I start getting ready for work." He sounded a little tired. "I want you to know, I won't be working on Christmas Eve," he said. "It sounds like your mother has a big fancy meal planned for all of us. Won't that be great? I'm looking forward to meeting Henry Dailey, too."

Danielle was surprised. "Henry Dailey is coming back here?"

"Yep, so I hear," Mr. Conners said. "He's down in Miami now, I believe. When your mother heard that both he and Alec would be here over the holiday, she insisted they join us for Christmas dinner."

Great, Danielle thought. *Grumpy old Henry Dailey.*

This was going to be some holiday.

CHAPTER TEN

Henry

As Christmas approached, Danielle realized that she'd have to face the fact that her days with Redman were numbered. She considered calling Mr. Sweet to beg him for extra time with her horse, but finally decided against it. She knew Mr. Sweet would insist that Redman be back in North Carolina by the beginning of the new year. To someone like Mr. Sweet, the beginning of the year meant *precisely* January first.

That's a week away, Danielle thought miserably. And not only would Redman's time at the farm be over soon, but she still had to figure out how to get the paint back up north. She'd kept pushing that problem out of her mind, hoping it would go away, but so far it hadn't. *I'd better start doing something before it's too late,* Danielle told herself. *Maybe Alec can help.*

She headed to the barn, where she found Alec

brushing out Raven. "Are you and Henry leaving your van down here?" she asked.

Alec looked up. "For the time being, I guess," he replied. "We're not going north again before the new year."

"Do you know of anyone who might be?" Danielle pressed.

"Well, let's see now," Alec said, continuing to brush, "This time of year, most of the horse traffic is coming down here from the farms up north."

Danielle nodded glumly.

"But if you're talking about getting Redman in a van to North Carolina, there might still be a way," Alec added.

"Really?" Danielle asked eagerly.

"With a little luck, you might be able to get him a ride with someone delivering a load of horses to South Wind who has to drive back north anyway."

"Do you really think so?" she said hopefully.

"Well, don't get your hopes up," said Alec. "But maybe. Just yesterday, someone from Maryland brought down a couple of colts. They dropped the horses off, then turned around and drove back empty. They would have given Reddy a ride, I bet."

"That'd be great!" exclaimed Danielle.

Alec held up his hands. "Now hold on, Danielle. I can't promise you anything, but I will keep my ears open."

"I understand, Alec," Danielle said. "I definitely won't count on anything, but whatever happens, it will all be worth it because I got to spend this time with Reddy." She didn't want Alec to think that she was ungrateful for his help in getting Redman home in the first place. And even if it cost her every cent of her savings to get Reddy back to Rocky Mount, she'd do it. A deal was a deal. And she still believed that her time with Redman was money well spent.

The paint was in the paddock, gently chewing on some grass. Dooley was perched nearby on the top fence rail, enjoying the sunshine. Slowly, Redman began to make his way along the fence. When he passed Dooley, the rooster dropped lightly onto his back to hitch a ride.

The rooster's bold move surprised Danielle, but Redman didn't even break stride as Dooley wobbled around on his back. The bird flapped his wings and crowed, then hopped off when Redman reached the next section of fence.

Alec came up behind Danielle as she was laughing at Dooley's antics. "Did you see that?" she asked.

"Yeah," said Alec, with a grin. "He pulled the same stunt yesterday. I think Reddy actually likes it."

Danielle climbed over the fence and headed toward the paddock gate to turn Redman loose in the lower pasture. As the paint trotted through the field, Danielle stood for a moment, watching her horse. It was going to be hard to let him go again, she thought. After a few minutes, she walked back to rejoin Alec, who was leaning against the fence. By now Dooley had hopped down from his perch and was exploring the driveway.

Alec and Danielle watched Redman run in the rolling gait that was uniquely his own. He lumbered, but at the same time the big paint was extremely graceful.

"It's funny how each horse's running style is different," Alec said as he gazed after Redman. "Their gait, their manner of stride—they all vary. And it's not about size or shape, either. Some horses that walk awkwardly can run beautifully. It's the same with people. Some people who are overweight can dance as lightly as a ballerina."

Danielle nodded, remembering something her mom had told her when they had gone jogging together once. "Think about the shape of peoples' bodies, Danielle," her mom had said. "We're all legs and arms, built to be in motion. We're not made to be sitting around all the time."

Alec and Danielle watched Redman prance around the pasture until a sound from the road made them both turn. A shiny green car was pulling into the driveway.

"That's Henry, I think," Alec said, glancing at his watch. Dooley scurried out of the car's way, squawking, as the car pulled to a stop beside the barn. The old trainer opened the door and stepped out. He was carrying an overnight bag.

Danielle followed Alec over to the car, feeling a little shy. Henry glanced at the two of them, then smiled at Dooley. It appeared as if he was in a good mood for once. "I don't remember seeing that bird when I was here before," he said.

"Oh, a friend of the family parked him here for a few days," said Alec. "He's made himself right at home. Dooley is his name."

"He'd be perfect for soup." Henry gave Danielle a wry smile when he saw her mouth drop open. "Only joking, kid. So how's the colt been?" Henry asked Alec, looking at the barn.

"Just fine," answered Alec. "Did everything go okay down in Miami?"

"I think so," Henry said. "We'll see if the man can do what he says." He left his overnight bag on the hood of the car and started for the barn. "Come on, I'd like to see Raven." Alec followed Henry, and after a moment's hesitation, so did Danielle.

Henry glanced around inside the barn and nodded in approval. Danielle had taken extra care in cleaning the place up that morning, and it showed. The trainer moved over to Raven's stall and peered in. After a moment, a broad smile swept across his wrinkled cheeks. He looked at Alec, his blue eyes sparkling excitedly, almost like a kid with a new toy.

"I think we might get lucky with this colt, Alec," he said. "We just might have ourselves a racehorse here."

Alec nodded. "That's exactly what I've been trying to tell you."

As Danielle listened to the two horsemen discuss the colt, she couldn't help feel a bit proud herself. After all, she'd spent more time with her Little Buddy than anyone else had so far in his young life.

"I'm warning you, though," Henry said, his excitement turning to earnestness. "We're going to have to be real careful with him. Plenty careful. We won't get any second chances with a horse like this."

"I know, Henry," Alec said, looking away.

Henry suddenly frowned. "Listen to me, son," he said sharply. "I've been in this racket all my life. I started with nothing, and I've done it all, from mucking out stalls and hustling mounts to training Derby winners. I've broken ribs, legs, arms, and even my nose in this game. I've paid my dues. And I'm standing here right now and saying that's as fine a colt as I've ever seen anywhere."

"He acts like he knows it sometimes," Alec said.

"Yeah? How's he coming along with his lessons?" Henry asked.

"Ask Danielle here," said Alec, nodding to her. "She had him out this morning."

Danielle felt Henry's piercing gaze turn on her. She straightened her shoulders a bit. "He's really doing well, I think, sir," she said.

"Good to hear," said Henry. "How's he getting along with that paint of yours?"

Danielle swallowed. "Umm...well, better. They still talk some, though." She glanced at Alec for a little help, but he was watching the colt move around the stall.

"Have you pastured them together yet?" Henry asked.

"No, sir," replied Danielle.

Henry shook his head in disapproval. "Well, don't you think it's about time? I mean, the colt's maturing fast physically, but what about his mind?"

Alec turned back to Henry. "Oh, the colt's pretty smart when he wants to be. But he still doesn't seem to know the difference between fighting and playing sometimes."

"You say he's still challenging the paint?"

Alec nodded. "He's just showing off, I think. I'm taking my time with him, though."

"Well, it's about time we pasture them together so we can see what's going on. The sooner we deal with this nonsense—"

"But what if they fight?" Danielle blurted out. "Sometimes Raven gets so wound up..."

The old trainer glared at Danielle, who suddenly

felt very sorry for interrupting him.

"This is my business, little lady. I know what I'm doing," scolded the trainer.

"Yes, sir," she said quietly.

Training horses might be your business, but Redman isn't some training tool for Raven, Danielle thought angrily. Redman was *her* horse.

At least for another week.

CHAPTER ELEVEN

Barnyard Rock

On Christmas Eve, Danielle gave both Raven and Redman extra rations of carrots, grain, and Texas hay to celebrate. After the horses were bedded down, she ran to the Coop to check in with Alec. He and Henry were playing cards at the kitchen table when she knocked on the door and peered inside.

"Need me for anything else?" she asked.

Alec looked up from his cards and smiled. "You go on home, Danielle," he said. "I'll look in on Raven a little later. We'll see you tomorrow, okay? Merry Christmas."

"Merry Christmas," Danielle called over her shoulder as she ran across the driveway toward her house.

A string of colored lights made the Conners home look extra cheery in the cool Florida night. The lights followed the edge of the roof and hung in tangled loops in the fronds of the palm tree by the door. Mr. Conners had tacked them up the day before, singing loudly during the whole process.

The house was quiet as Danielle entered. The only thing she could hear was the radio playing a country-and-western version of a Christmas carol.

"Danielle? Is that you?" her mom called from the kitchen.

"It's me, Mom."

"Get cleaned up and come in here and give me a hand peeling these potatoes, okay?"

"Sure," said Danielle. She ran to the bathroom and washed her hands. The whole family would be sitting down to a big dinner by noon the next day, so Danielle knew that her mom was getting as much of it ready tonight as possible. They were supposed to go to midnight Mass, too, so they didn't have much time left to prepare.

Danielle spent the next hour cutting carrots, peeling potatoes, and opening cans of cranberry sauce. Mrs. Conners made a couple pans of gingerbread cookies that Danielle decorated with sprinkles, cinnamon buttons, and walnut hats. Soon the kitchen was filled with wonderful holiday cooking smells.

Mr. Conners and Dylan came home from gathering firewood, and they all changed into their best clothes and loaded into the car for the drive to church. Midnight Mass was in the new church on the other side of Wishing Wells. Danielle was looking forward to everyone singing and to seeing all the candles lit up. Going to Mass in the nighttime made it special, too.

By the time they got home, it was pretty late. Danielle and Dylan left milk and cookies out for Santa Claus.

"Now make sure you get to sleep fast," their mom told them, "so that Santa can come down and leave nice presents for you."

"Hey, we forgot to leave anything for the King," Dylan said after her mother left.

"Dad's making some popcorn, I think," Danielle said.

"I could use a jelly doughnut myself about now."

Danielle laughed. The King, of course, was Elvis Presley, at least around the Conners household. Their father had shown up in costume with a sack of presents one Christmas Eve a couple years ago, scaring her and Dylan half to death. Ever since then, the family always left doughnuts or a big bowl of popcorn out for the King on Christmas Eve, in case he had to fill in for Santa again.

The next morning, Danielle woke up before anyone else and ran downstairs to the living room. Faint beams of early morning sunlight were filtering in under the window shade. Among the presents piled under the tree was a new red saddle blanket that Danielle guessed was for her and Redman.

"All right, Santa!" she cried, grabbing the blanket. She looked around for other presents, but didn't really think she would find many there for her. This year she knew that her big present, Redman, was out in the barn waiting for his breakfast.

Danielle checked her Christmas stocking and found candy canes, an orange, and a huge bar of chocolate. She took one of the candy canes and quietly opened the front door, tucking the new blanket under her arm to show Reddy.

The barn was still in shadows as she stepped inside and walked over to Redman's stall. The paint was waiting for her with his head hung over the half door. He murmured softly as she reached for the latch.

Suddenly a sharp *Er-er-RUH* broke through the stillness. But it wasn't coming from Dooley's pen. It was coming from Raven's stall.

What in the world has that rooster done now? thought Danielle.

She rushed to Raven's stall. In the shadows, she could see Dooley perched on the door. Inside the stall, Raven started shrilling and whinnying. Then Redman joined in. In seconds, the whole barn was going full blast, the animals giving their own version of caroling in the cool Christmas morning.

How did Dooley get out of his pen? Danielle wondered. *And what* is *he doing messing around with Raven?* Danielle knew that Redman might put up with Dooley's antics. But Raven was another story. The colt was so high-strung and moody these days that she could never tell whether he was in a playful mood or not. All it would take was one well-placed throw of a hoof and a certain crazy rooster would end up with more than a broken wing.

"Get down from there," Danielle called to Dooley. The bird was balancing lightly on the edge of the door. He started flapping his wings when he saw Danielle approaching. Raven shrilled again.

She heard quick footsteps coming into the barn behind her. "What's all the fuss about, Danielle?" Alec asked, sounding worried.

Er-er-RUH, crowed Dooley.

Danielle looked around helplessly. Before she could grab him, the rooster quickly made his escape, jumping down and scurrying away. Inside his stall, Raven bellowed some more. Then Redman answered back. Danielle and Alec both looked at Raven and then turned to each other. A smile broke across Alec's face.

"Well, Merry Christmas morning to you, too," he called to the colt.

"Dooley must have slipped loose from his pen again," Danielle said. "I'm sorry. I couldn't catch him."

"No harm done," Alec said calmly, unlatching Raven's stall. "Did you give Redman his breakfast yet?"

Danielle shook her head.

"I'll take care of this guy," Alec said. "You take care of Redman, okay?"

"Sounds good," Danielle said. "Are we really going to try turning him and Raven out together?"

Alec nodded. "Henry thinks it's time."

"What do *you* think?" Danielle asked cautiously.

"If Henry thinks it's time, it's time," Alec answered. "The paddock is neutral territory. Henry wants to start there first."

"Today?" Danielle asked warily. She had a bad feeling about this.

"Why not?"

"But it's Christmas," Danielle said.

Alec shrugged. "The horses don't know that. We'll see what Henry says later. Hey, by the way, Merry Christmas, Danielle."

"Thanks, Alec. Merry Christmas to you, too," she said. *Should I have gotten him a present?* she wondered.

Danielle went over to Redman's stall. She wasn't all that anxious to see her horse used as a guinea pig to test Raven's social skills. But maybe it wouldn't be so bad, she hoped. With pros like Henry and Alec to oversee things, it couldn't get *too* bad.

She didn't want to pester Alec, but she really

wanted to ask him again about any vans coming to South Wind that might be able to take Redman back to North Carolina. She figured that Alec probably would have mentioned it to her if he'd heard of anything. But just the same, she couldn't help worrying.

Dooley's crowing interrupted Danielle's thoughts for a moment. In a way, she was thankful for Dooley's antics. If nothing else, the rooster's mischief-making had distracted the two horses from their feud. Danielle laughed and shook her head. *Life in the barn sure can be funny sometimes,* she thought.

Redman was still a bit worked up from his early-morning caroling and was pacing in his stall when Danielle went inside. He snorted and came over to her right away, nudging her pockets. She suddenly remembered the candy cane she'd found in her stocking. Digging it out of her pocket, she broke it into pieces and gave one to Reddy. Then she gave herself a treat, popping a piece in her own mouth. She took off Redman's old saddle blanket and draped the new one over his back. "Merry Christmas, Reddy," she said.

Redman seemed pleased with his present. He happily crunched up his peppermint while Danielle started getting his breakfast ready. She hummed the first few bars of "Jingle Bell Rock" to herself as she worked.

So far, it was a great Christmas.

CHAPTER TWELVE

Holiday Truce

Christmas dinner at Danielle's house was always a little crazy. This year was no exception. All afternoon Dylan kept playing scratchy old 78-rpm records on the ancient turntable Mom and Dad had gotten him. Danielle's new bead-jewelry-making kit had spilled on the floor, and Mr. Conners had almost broken his neck when he slipped on one of the beads.

"Danielle!" Mrs. Conners called from the kitchen.

"Coming, Mom," Danielle answered. She was carrying dishes of food out to the dining room. Dylan was setting the table. Grandma Conners had already arrived and was helping Mrs. Conners in the kitchen. Danielle's dad, Clyde Katz, Alec, and Henry sat in the living room talking. Wrapping paper and ribbons were scattered on the floor under the Christmas tree. Newly opened gifts were still lying around, too.

"Get some pot holders and take this," Mrs.

Conners said when Danielle stepped back into the kitchen. She handed Danielle a steaming bowl of spicy-smelling sweet potatoes.

"I love the way Grandma makes sweet potatoes," Danielle said. "Do you think there's going to be enough?"

"There's plenty more on the stove," Mrs. Conners answered. "And don't you dare stick your finger in that bowl."

Just as Danielle's mom called everyone to dinner, Grandma Conners slipped Danielle an envelope.

"It's a little extra this year, Danny," she said. "I know how tough it's been for you and your horse. I hope this will help a bit."

Danielle gave her a big hug. "Thank you, Grandma," she said, and Grandma Conners affectionately patted her on the back.

They sat down to eat. The table was set with a big white tablecloth and red-and-green holiday place mats. Mr. Conners sat at the head, carving the turkey. Mrs. Conners stood beside him, holding the plates and passing them on once they were full. Everyone piled on mashed potatoes, stuffing, cranberry sauce, and lots of gravy. It was a grand feast. Danielle sat between Clyde and her grandma. Her brother sat across from her, with Alec and Henry on either side of him. The two horsemen were talking about Raven.

"The colt sure is a lot bigger than when I saw him a couple months ago," commented Mr. Conners.

"He's bigger, all right," Henry replied, "and a little too full of himself. Alec's been babying him."

Alec chuckled. "Now, Henry. Raven's a good boy, you know it."

"He's a hard-headed colt that needs to learn some manners," Henry said.

As the adults continued their discussion, Dylan started goofing off, teetering back on his chair and twirling his fork around in his fingers. Something went wrong, however, when he tried passing the fork from one hand to the other. Like a guided missile it flew out of his hand, scoring a direct hit on Henry's mashed potatoes!

"Dylan!" Mr. Conners said sternly.

"Oops. Sorry." Dylan said.

Henry shook his head and calmly returned Dylan's fork. "Looks like Raven isn't the only young colt around here that needs to learn some stable manners." Everyone had a good laugh at Dylan's expense.

Alec reached over and gave half his serving of meat to Dylan. Grandma Conners watched the transaction and raised an eyebrow. "Don't you like turkey, Alec?" she asked.

Alec smiled. "If I put it on now, I'll just have to work twice as hard to get it off later," he said. "As a jockey, I'm always having to make weight."

Grandma shook her head. "It's hard to believe anything could keep a healthy young man from filling up on good turkey at Christmas time."

As they ate and talked, Clyde told a story about the place that the band played in the night before. "There was some loud guy who started making wisecracks during the set," Clyde said. "He was making fun of your daddy's earring, saying that *real* country singers don't wear earrings. Poor guy didn't know who he was talking to, I guess, because some friends of your dad's were in the audience, and they were big. A couple of them were getting ready to take the dumb son of a gun out back and—"

"Clyde," Mr. Conners interrupted. "Come on, now. It's Christmas."

"Needless to say, it was quite a brouhaha," Clyde told Danielle, sneaking in some last words.

"Not quite so dramatic as that. Mostly we just cranked up the volume so we couldn't hear them!" Mr. Conners said, laughing. "That's standard operating procedure for dealing with hecklers."

By the end of the meal, everyone was stuffed. Alec had even managed to put away two pieces of pumpkin pie and a bowl of ice cream despite his diet.

Grandma nodded at one of the unfinished pies. "Sure you don't want another piece?"

Alec pushed back from the table and patted his stomach. "No, thanks."

"Eat," Grandma insisted. "It's a holiday."

Alec smiled and shook his head. "Thanks. But I must say that is some of the best pumpkin pie I've ever had, except for my mom's, of course."

"You said your folks are out in California now?" Grandma asked.

"Yes, ma'am," Alec said.

"Don't you miss your family?"

"I'll be seeing them soon," Alec said. "Besides, Henry's here, and the horses. They're my family too, these days."

Eventually everyone got up from the table and slowly made their way into the living room. Mr. Conners carried cups of coffee from the kitchen. He chuckled to himself as he noticed that Henry was falling asleep on the couch.

"Looks like Henry could have used some of this," Mr. Conners said as he placed the cups on the table.

"Just as long as he doesn't start snoring," Alec said.

A while later, he woke Henry up, and the two of them said their thanks and went back to the Coop. Grandma also wanted to get home before it got too late. Danielle and Dylan each gave her a big hug before she left.

When the guests were gone and the dishes were done, Danielle changed into jeans and a sweatshirt and ran out to the barn to visit Redman. On her way, she saw Raven in the pasture, snoozing under a tree.

Danielle picked up some brushes in the tack room and found Redman nosing around the hay rack in his stall. The paint looked very handsome under his new red stable blanket. He whinnied when he saw Danielle.

"Hey, Reddy," Danielle called as she slipped in beside her horse.

She gave him some carrots left over from dinner and then set to work giving him a quick grooming. She heard Dooley crowing outside the barn as well as Alec laughing. Then the rooster crowed even louder. Danielle left Redman chomping the last bit of candy cane she'd had in her pocket and went out to see what was up.

Alec was making a halfhearted effort to chase the rooster, who had somehow gotten loose again. Dooley ducked under the paddock fence.

Alec threw up his hands in defeat and came over to Danielle.

"Hey, Alec," Danielle said, handing him an envelope covered in sparkling green-and-red wrapping paper. "I forgot to give you this before."

Alec took the envelope, looking a bit embarrassed. "Thanks, Danielle. That's very kind of you," he said, and ripped open the package.

"It's just a kitchen magnet, but I thought you'd like it." Alec held up the small horse-head-shaped magnet. Danielle had found the last-minute gift for Alec among the junk in her bottom desk drawer.

"This is great," Alec said with a shy smile. "Now let me see, what do I have for you?" He started for the barn. "Come here a second."

Danielle followed Alec into the barn and over to Raven's tack trunk. He opened the lid and started digging around under some folded stable sheets. "There it is," he said, pulling out a brown paper bag and handing it to her. "Pardon the wrapping."

Danielle opened her present. It was a T-shirt from last year's Kentucky Derby!

"Wow," Danielle said.

"Do you like it?" Alec asked.

"It's terrific. Really cool. Thanks." They both left their presents in the tack room and walked out to the paddock again.

"So, how's Redman?" Alec asked. "Aren't you going to turn him out today?"

"I was just about to," said Danielle. *Sort of,* she added to herself. She knew what Alec was going to say next.

"Let me bring Raven to the paddock first," he said. "Henry wants to see if Raven behaves around Redman. We might as well see what happens now.

Danielle gulped. "Now?"

"Might as well," Alec said again. "Don't worry, Danielle. Everything will be okay." He fetched a halter and lead line from the tack room and then went to retrieve Raven from the pasture.

Danielle heard the door to the Coop slam shut. She turned and saw Henry Dailey hitching up his pants as he walked toward the barn. He stopped beside the fence rail where Danielle was standing.

"Fine dinner you and your mother made, Danielle," Henry said, still sounding a little sleepy. "I haven't eaten that well in a long time."

"Thank you. I'm glad you enjoyed it," Danielle said politely.

"I sure did," said Henry as he patted his stomach contentedly. Danielle smiled. What a funny guy Henry Dailey was, she thought. He could be warm and friendly one minute and snap your head off the next, especially when he was around horses.

The old trainer and Danielle watched Alec chasing Raven around the pasture. The colt was feeling a bit frisky, prancing one way and then tearing off toward the opposite fence. Henry turned to Danielle, a half-proud, half-eager expression crossing his face.

"Look at that stride," Henry said excitedly, gazing back out into the pasture. "Look at all that daylight under him when he moves out. It's amazing."

Alec was finally able to catch the colt and get a

lead line on him. The two of them started back to the barn. Once they were inside the paddock, Henry and Danielle slipped through the gate. Raven was dancing at the end of his lead line, while Alec kept up a singsong murmuring, trying to keep the colt calm.

Henry stood in front of Raven and firmly took hold of his halter. He stared deep into the horse's eyes. Then the trainer stepped back and moved slowly around the colt, inspecting him from top to bottom. Every once in a while he gave a satisfied grunt.

Danielle's stomach dropped. *Uh-oh,* she thought. *I have a bad feeling about this. What if...?*

"Okay," said Henry. "Let's bring out the paint."

CHAPTER THIRTEEN

Battle for Attention

Danielle hurried to the tack room to find a lead shank. She wasn't at all anxious to see a confrontation between her two favorite horses. And she didn't like the look that she had just seen in Raven's eye. If the decision had been up to her, Danielle would have kept them apart for the rest of Redman's visit. They were doing just fine in their separate pastures. Redman had to go back to North Carolina in less than a week, so why not just leave them alone?

This is something Alec and Henry want, she told herself. *They consider this part of Raven's training.* Although she wanted to tell Henry and Alec that she thought they were wrong, she knew they were the professionals, not she. She'd have to go along with their experiment.

Redman heard Danielle rustling around in the tack room and poked his head above the half doors as she came into the barn to get him. He had an expectant expression on his face, as if he knew something was up.

Danielle brought Redman out of his stall and walked him down the aisle toward the paddock. "Good boy," she said. "How's my guy? You look so fine today."

Out in the paddock, Raven was starting to buck and play. Alec held him as still as he could. As Danielle led Redman closer, the colt began to whinny. The paint stopped short, bracing his legs. Then he snorted and started pawing the ground.

Oh, boy, thought Danielle. *This is not going to be fun.*

"Come on," Henry said impatiently, waving Danielle ahead. "Bring that horse in here!" he ordered.

Raven snorted at Redman. Danielle took a deep breath, gripped the lead tightly in her hands, and urged Redman ahead. The two horses eyed each other cautiously. Raven tossed his head around, trying to look tough. Henry grinned. "He's just playing, trying to see how much he can get away with," the trainer said.

But Danielle wasn't so sure. She knew Raven pretty well, and she still didn't trust the look in his eyes. Alec beckoned for her to bring Redman even closer. Moments later, the two horses were face-to-face.

Raven glared at Redman, but neither horse

backed away. Redman watched the colt, swinging his head back and forth as if he was uninterested.

"Easy now," Alec said softly.

Redman turned toward Danielle, ignoring the colt.

Maybe this won't be so bad after all, Danielle thought. Alec and Henry were both there. The horses were on lead lines. Even if Raven wanted to start anything, it wouldn't be easy for him. Alec had him in short hold on the lead and was turning him in a tight circle. Raven was up on his toes, ready to go, but he wasn't really getting out of hand.

Alec shook his head. "This colt is all business, I'm telling you. *His* business," he said. "He demands attention practically every second. I wonder if we'll ever be able to relax with him."

"He'll settle down," Henry said. "But he'll never be the kind of horse a jockey can let his guard down with."

Alec took an even shorter hold on the lead. "He's a lot like the Black, I think. It's more a matter of learning when you can trust him and when that would be...dangerous."

"Well," Henry said, "the only way to find out is by observing him."

He stepped in beside Raven and started unfastening the colt's halter. Then he nodded at Danielle. "Turn the paint loose, too."

Nervously, Danielle did as Henry said. Redman

glanced at her and bobbed his head as she fumbled with the halter. Finally, she slipped it off his head, but kept her hand on her horse's neck.

Raven started to back up. "Easy, boy," said Alec.

"Let them go," Henry ordered.

Suddenly, the colt shrilled and whirled, letting fly his hind hooves.

Alec jumped out of the way just in time. Henry staggered backward and almost fell over. Danielle sprang back, and Redman slipped away from her. Henry quickly recovered his balance, even before Alec and Danielle did. In a flash, the old trainer was after the horses.

Together, the black colt and the big paint sidestepped to the other side of the paddock. Snorting and whinnying and carrying on, they circled each other like two big wrestlers about to square off.

"The gate!" Henry shouted over his shoulder. "Open the gate!"

Alec quickly turned and ran for the paddock gate.

Raven whirled, letting fly with his hooves again. This time, he aimed directly at Redman. Danielle screamed, but the paint saw the hooves coming and dodged out of the way. Danielle gasped. If the blow had landed, it would have sent the older horse reeling.

Redman shifted his weight back onto his

haunches. Then, he rose up, pawing the air, and brought his forefeet crashing to the ground beside the colt. Henry jerked the hat off his head and sprang forward, waving his arms and trying to get between the two horses. The black colt and the paint were screaming at each other, their bodies shaking.

"Whoa, *whoa!*" Henry ordered sharply. His voice barely rose above the cries of the raging horses.

Danielle stood on the balls of her feet, ready to move into action but not knowing what to do. She wanted to scream again, but held her tongue. The last thing this situation needed was more screaming. She just wished she could help somehow.

Suddenly, another jarring voice joined the commotion. It was Dooley coming to see what all the excitement was about.

Er-er-RUH! crowed the big-tailed rooster. He skittered along the fence and then bumbled into the paddock to watch the two horses stand off.

Danielle couldn't believe it. Now, on top of everything else, this crazy bird was involved, too. She chased Dooley, trying to get him out of the way. But he was too quick for her.

Everything was in total chaos now. The horses had outflanked Henry and were stalking each other up and down the paddock. The rooster dodged this way and that, managing to slip past Danielle and get himself into the thick of the action. Alec opened the paddock gate and came running back to help, but Dooley seemed to enjoy dancing between Redman and Raven. He crowed like mad, dodged hooves, and missed getting trampled by inches. Then the undaunted rooster hopped up on the top fence rail and crowed at both horses.

Danielle started to run toward Redman, but Alec stopped her. "Stay back," he said. "It's too dangerous."

Just as Alec finished speaking, Raven spun on Redman again and reared up. The paint pulled back and started to wheel around, threatening to throw out his hind hooves. Raven was about to turn on Redman again when the rooster suddenly hopped from his perch onto the colt's back! The lunatic bird moved quickly and easily, as if he had been riding Raven for years. Danielle's mouth dropped open in shock.

"Well, I'll be," Henry muttered softly in disbelief.

It took a second for the raging colt to realize he was suddenly carrying a passenger.

Dooley continued crowing. *Er-er-RUH.*

Danielle and Alec exchanged worried glances. No one—nothing—had ever been on Raven's back before. The colt's eyes shifted wildly in his head.

Er-er-RUH crowed the big-tailed bird again, standing tall and proud on the colt's back. Raven forgot all about Redman and started bucking to get rid of the unwelcome hitchhiker.

Danielle took advantage of the distraction to move in closer to Redman. *If I can just get him to listen to me or get him through the paddock gate as an escape route...*she thought.

Dooley hung on like a rodeo pro for a few moments, and then skipped off Raven's back and skittered under the fence rails. In the confusion, Alec got to Raven's head and laid his hands on the colt.

"Easy, boy, easy," he called to the colt with soft, low commands.

Redman bolted for the paddock gate, and Danielle chased after him. She caught up to her horse halfway up the driveway. When she put her hand on his neck, he did not shy from her. His blowing and snorting lessened after a moment or two.

"Where you going, Reddy?" said Danielle. "Don't worry, this is your home. Please don't be mad at me about Raven. He's really not so bad, he's just..."

He's just what? thought Danielle. The colt was acting like a spoiled brat. If it hadn't been for Dooley's antics, one of the horses could have been seriously hurt.

"Oh, Reddy," she said shakily, tears pricking her eyes. "You're okay, and that's all that matters." The big paint dropped his head and shuddered.

Danielle walked along beside him, not really sure why any of this needed to have happened.

"Please understand, Reddy," she sighed, slipping her hand up her horse's sweaty neck. "This wasn't my idea."

She just hoped Redman could understand. And maybe forgive her.

CHAPTER FOURTEEN

Questions

Back at the paddock, Henry and Alec were still trying to get Raven settled down. Once the colt was finally under control, they led him into the barn to his stall. Danielle turned Reddy loose in the upper pasture, then returned to the paddock. Dooley was nowhere to be seen. Henry and Alec were laughing when they came out of the barn. The old trainer shook his head. "How about that ol' bird joining the party?"

Alec smiled. "I don't know if the colt is going to be too anxious to tangle with Dooley again."

This is too much, Danielle thought. *They're actually laughing about what just happened.* That made her really angry, especially at Alec. He knew how she felt about Redman, and Raven, too. This wasn't some big joke to her.

"Is Raven okay?" Danielle asked seriously.

Henry glanced at her briefly. "He's just fine."

"I was really afraid someone might get hurt," Danielle said.

"You did all right back there, kid," said Henry. "You didn't lose your head. It's not an easy thing to do in a situation like that. Anyway, we got a good start."

"Start?" Danielle said. She couldn't believe she was hearing this. "You mean you're gonna do this again?"

"Why not?" Henry said. "Everything we just went through will be a waste if we don't."

Danielle was doing her best to hide her anger, but it wasn't easy. She stood there not knowing what to say.

"No need to worry, Danielle," Alec said, finally seeming to realize how Danielle was feeling. "We won't let Reddy get hurt. Everything is under control."

Danielle wasn't so sure. *You said that last time,* she wanted to say. But judging from Alec's serious expression, she could tell that Alec was certain of it. "I know, Alec," she said slowly. "It's not like I don't trust you. But Redman is still *my* horse. What if he gets hurt?"

"It'll go better next time," Alec said softly. "You'll see."

Alec's confidence made Danielle feel a little better, though not much. "It's just that...well, Reddy's only going to be here for a few more days," she said, "and I still don't know how I'm going to get him back north to Sweet's camp again."

"I'm sorry, Danielle," Alec said, taking the hint. "There aren't as many horse vans going north from South Wind as I thought there would be. I'll keep asking around, though. Maybe something will turn up."

Danielle nodded and looked over to see Redman capering off through the pasture. Time was quickly running out. In a few days, Danielle would be stuck without a way to get Reddy back to North Carolina. Twice a day Mom and Dad seemed to be reminding her of that fact. *What will Mr. Sweet do if I can't deliver on my promise to return Redman after the holidays?* wondered Danielle. *I'll be lucky to even see Reddy again, much less get Mr. Sweet to sell him back to me someday.*

Alec and Henry walked off by themselves, talking in whispers. Henry was staring out into the pasture at Redman. *This is Henry's fault,* Danielle thought angrily. *Alec would never make me use Reddy as a sparring partner for Raven. Especially with the little time I have left with him.*

Suddenly, an unsettling thought struck her. She had always assumed that Alec had offered his help to get Redman home for the holidays as a favor to her. But maybe he really had been thinking about Raven instead. Maybe using Redman to help socialize Raven had been part of Alec's plan all along.

Danielle felt a wave of fury inside her, but she knew there was no point in getting angry. She knew that no matter what the answer was, there wasn't much she could do about the situation. Alec and Henry *were* professional horsemen with a future championship racehorse. And she was just a kid with a big old paint.

"Danielle!" Mrs. Conners called. Danielle turned and saw her mother waving from the porch. She jogged back to the house.

"Uncle Ray's on the phone," Mrs. Conners said. "He wants to wish you a Merry Christmas. What was all that ruckus with the horses?"

"You mean you didn't see it?" Danielle asked.

"No, honey. I was taking a nap," Mrs. Conners said. "I figured Alec and Henry had things under control."

Danielle was shocked. "I can't believe you could sleep through that!"

"Are you kidding?" Mrs. Conners said. "After all that work in the kitchen, I could have slept through anything. Maybe if I had had a little more help cleaning up..."

"Sorry, Mom. But Raven and Reddy were about to fight," Danielle said. "Dooley jumped on Raven's back. It was a total mess."

Mrs. Conners motioned to the kitchen phone.

"Danielle, I think you'd better get to Uncle Ray."

"All right, I'll tell you about it later," said Danielle, a little annoyed that her mom didn't seem interested.

Didn't anyone care but her?

The next afternoon Henry and Alec worked Redman and Raven together in the same paddock again. This time there were no fireworks, just a lot of huffing and puffing. Danielle still didn't like it. *What's the point?* she thought. *Raven and Redman aren't going to be stabled together very long.* This was all about Raven. And she had other things on her mind right now.

Her dad was leaving town for a few days to play a gig in Jacksonville. At breakfast, before he left and her mom went off to work, the two of them had started lecturing her about Redman and Mr. Sweet and "being responsible." This was *her* problem, her parents said. They wanted her to work it out herself.

To make matters worse, Dylan was driving her nuts playing his old 78s at full volume. And Dooley wasn't helping much, either. Once again, that crazy bird had managed to slip the latch on his cage and fly around the barnyard, eventually making his way into the paddock to ride around on Redman. Dooley wasn't quite crazy enough to jump up on Raven's back again, Danielle noticed. He still managed to pester Raven in other ways, though, like dodging around his feet when Raven wasn't looking.

"You know, I think that rooster is helping cool things down around here as much as we are," Alec told Danielle later that afternoon. They were both leaning on the paddock fence, watching Dooley strut across the driveway.

"Yeah, he certainly has given Raven something to think about besides Reddy," Danielle said.

As her gaze followed Dooley, her thoughts returned to her number-one problem: how to get Redman north. She had already called the only two horse-transport companies she could find in the phone book, and their prices were ridiculous. The best deal was from some guy her mom had heard about. But that wasn't much of a bargain, either. Even if she used her entire Redman savings fund, it would barely cover half the cost of trucking Reddy north. And she couldn't ask her parents for help. The whole family was broke, even with her dad doing extra gigs over the holidays.

Unfortunately, Alec's tips on vans at South Wind were leading nowhere. "I'm sorry, Danielle. I didn't mean to get your hopes up," he'd said the last time she'd asked. "But I'll keep trying. I promise. I even have Henry asking around."

Redman was in the pasture now, relaxing after their morning ride. She walked out to see him again.

"Now I'm really stuck, Reddy," Danielle told her horse with a sigh. "How am I ever going to get you up north again? I guess it was a stupid idea, bringing you home like this with no way to get you back. I was so sure it would work out. And Mr. Sweet is expecting you in just a few days."

She stroked Redman's neck. The big paint bobbed his head sympathetically.

They stood together in silence, gazing off at the horizon. A fresh breeze blew in from the north.

So far, Danielle thought, they had a whole bunch of questions and no answers.

CHAPTER FIFTEEN

Last Ride

"I'm really getting desperate," Danielle told her mom as they sat at the kitchen table after dinner. "Redman is supposed to be back at Mr. Sweet's in three days." Mrs. Conners was drinking coffee, and Danielle was playing with a bowl of melting ice cream.

Danielle's mom shook her head. "I don't know what to tell you, Danielle. You're already aware of how your father and I feel about the situation."

"Yes, Mom," Danielle said with a sigh.

"What did Alec say?" Mrs. Conners asked.

"He told me he's still asking around South Wind for vans going north."

"That's all?"

Danielle shrugged. "I guess."

"Well, you are the one who's supposed to be doing something," Mrs. Conners said firmly. "You're responsible, Danielle. Redman is your horse, and you made another crazy deal with Mr. Sweet."

"I know, Mom." *Here we go again,* Danielle thought. Her parents were very big on responsibility.

Mrs. Conners took another sip of coffee. "And if you can't handle this problem, then you're going to have to ask Alec to help pay for Redman's trip back."

"Come on, Mom," said Danielle. "I can't do that."

"Well, if you won't, I will."

"No, please," Danielle said.

"Why not?"

"I was the one who promised Mr. Sweet that I'd have Reddy back by the new year," Danielle said. "Maybe I can borrow the money somewhere to ship Reddy north."

"From where, honey?"

Danielle shrugged. "I don't know. A bank, maybe?"

Mrs. Conners laughed. "Right. Find me a bank that will lend their money to a twelve-year-old girl. And don't even *think* about asking your grandma. She's given us enough already."

"I'm not asking Grandma for money," Danielle said.

Mrs. Conners touched Danielle on the arm and looked her straight in the eye. "Alec is the only one left, Danielle. You'll just have to ask him to help you out. Unless you have a better idea, of course."

Danielle didn't. She felt trapped. "Okay," she

heard herself say, "I'll ask him. Tomorrow. I promise."

"Tomorrow, then," Mrs. Conners said. "And if you start thinking about changing your mind, remember that your dad is coming home tomorrow night. Maybe he should speak with Alec about this."

Oh, please! Danielle thought. *Anything but that. How embarrassing.*

When Danielle woke up the next morning, she almost felt like running away. But running off with Redman was one of the reasons she was in this situation now.

By the time she dressed and got out to the barn, Alec had already left for South Wind. Henry was taking some horses to the track and wanted to get an early start. There was a note on the clipboard telling Danielle what to do with Raven. It also said that Alec would be back that afternoon.

Danielle felt a little relieved. At least now she could wait until later to talk to Alec about helping her with Redman. Inside the barn, Raven and Redman were both awake, whinnying for their breakfast.

"All right, you guys," Danielle said. "I'm coming."

She went from stall to stall, feeding the horses and cleaning out their bedding. Then she turned them out. Reddy went into the upper pasture and Raven into the lower.

The way things had begun to change between the two horses was truly amazing, thought Danielle. Yesterday Henry and Alec had even pastured Raven and Redman together for a while, with hardly a word between them. *I guess they were right,* she told herself. She would have never believed it would be possible a few days ago. Whatever had made Raven act the crazy way he had seemed to be gone from his system.

Danielle watched the two horses running around for a moment. Would Raven and Redman have turned out to be friends anyway? she wondered. Or had they really needed help?

She went back into the barn to finish cleaning up. On the way, she stopped by Dooley's cage and threw him a few handfuls of grain. "Guess I owe you one," she told him. The rooster strutted about his pen, squawking and flapping his wings. Danielle smiled. *Crazy bird,* she thought.

After Danielle finished getting the barn in order, she worked Raven on the lead line a while, just as Alec had requested in his note. Returning Raven to his stall, she started to sweep out the barn aisle. As

Danielle worked, she thought about what she was going to say when she saw Alec. Could she really confront him as her mom had suggested? Did she even have a choice? Should she wait? What if she asked for a loan against her future pay?

She walked outside to find Redman. He was standing by the pasture fence, looking lonely. *Forget it,* she thought. *I'll figure it out later.* Right now, she and Redman were going for a ride.

A few minutes later, Reddy was saddled up and ready to go. As they reached the dirt road above their neighbors' cow pasture, Danielle encouraged him into a gallop. But the paint was acting frisky and really wanted to run. When she started tugging on his mouth to get him to slow down, he galloped faster, his mane streaming.

Danielle leaned forward onto her horse's neck. "Easy, boy. Easy," she whispered. "Not so fast." She almost lost a stirrup. For a few seconds, she could only hold on and hope to ride out his pounding gallop.

When she found her seat again, she hauled on the reins until Redman finally slowed down. "What was *that* all about?" Danielle asked her horse as they slowed to a jolting walk. "It's not like you." The paint just snorted and tossed his head.

They stopped after a while in a field above the woods. Danielle took an apple from her jacket pocket and held it out to Redman. He blinked at her, bit the apple in half, and then spit it out into Danielle's hand. Then he turned and started to walk away.

"What's the matter? Aren't you hungry?" she asked, confused. "Since when don't you like apples?"

When Redman noticed that Danielle wasn't following, he turned back and seemed to beckon with his head.

"Where are you going?" she called after him as she followed her horse through the pasture. *Might as well let him get this out of his system,* she told herself.

Redman walked toward a patch of green grass on one side of a big shady oak tree. Both he and Danielle knew the spot well. It was one of their favorite places to rest and relax after a ride in the woods. Redman waited for her there. She walked up to him and offered him the other half of the apple. The paint lowered his head and took it. As he munched, she put her arm around his neck, giving her horse a hug.

Is Reddy going to miss me? she wondered. *Does he know how mixed-up I feel?*

They lingered at the tree a while longer. Then they rode over to the marl pits and down around the canal. Danielle wished the ride could last forever.

She still had no idea what she should do when

they got back. Alec had been so nice to help her get Reddy down to Florida for the holidays. She just knew that she would feel guilty asking him for help. Besides, how was she ever going to get Alec to take her seriously if she kept acting like a little kid all the time, throwing up her hands and saying "Help me!"

Luckily, Redman decided not to act up on the ride back to the farm. He barely broke a slow trot the whole time.

When they cleared the ridge overlooking the farm, Danielle saw that Alec was already back. He was working Raven in circles at the end of a lead line down in the pasture. *This is it,* Danielle told herself. *I'd better talk to Alec now before...*Suddenly, she spotted her dad's car in the driveway. *Oh, no! He's not supposed to be home until tonight!* Danielle thought wildly. The last thing she wanted was for her parents to talk to Alec about Redman before she did. If that happened, she would really feel like an idiot.

She could just make out the people on the porch. Her mom and dad and someone else. It looked like a woman.

Leaving Redman in the paddock, she pulled off his saddle and tack and carried it into the barn. When she came back outside, her dad waved from the porch.

"Danny!" he called. "Come here."

Danielle ran over and jogged up the porch steps. Her dad and mom were sitting in porch chairs, drinking coffee. "Good news," Mr. Conners said, smiling broadly. "I think we've found your horse a ride north."

CHAPTER SIXTEEN

A Holiday Miracle

Oh, no, Danielle though. *My parents have already talked to Alec!* Her heart dropped. The woman sitting on the wicker couch beside Danielle's parents smiled at her. She looked about sixty years old. She offered Danielle her hand and gave her a friendly squeeze.

"Danielle," said Mr. Conners, "this is Mrs. Leslie Loon, the woman who works with Dooley."

Dooley's owner? Isn't she supposed to be in the hospital? Danielle wondered.

"Pleased to meet you, ma'am," she said aloud.

"Hiya, pumpkin," said Mrs. Loon in a deep, scratchy voice. She wore enough jewelry for ten people, with dangly gold earrings, rings on practically every finger, and a gold watch on her wrist. Her shirt was a bright red-and-green tropical print, and she wore white running shoes on her feet. Danielle noticed a piece of gauze bandage sticking out from under her left sleeve. She looked pretty good for someone who'd just been in a car crash, Danielle thought.

"Your daddy rescued me from the hospital just in time," Mrs. Loon said. "I was about to jump out the window." She looked over at Mr. Conners and smiled.

Danielle's dad smiled back and shook his head. "You didn't sound like you were going to be jumping anywhere when I talked to you last week."

Mrs. Loon made a face and waved her hand. "Well, it was a fine place to spend Christmas, laid up in a hospital bed." She took a sip of her coffee.

"Um, Dad," Danielle asked, "what did you just say about Redman? About a ride north? Did you talk to Alec already?"

Mr. Conners didn't reply right away. He glanced at Danielle's mom, then at Mrs. Loon.

"Leslie says she can give Redman a ride," Mr. Conners said. "She's going north."

Danielle looked back and forth between her dad and Leslie Loon. She couldn't believe her luck.

"Wow, you mean it? You're really going north?" she asked Mrs. Loon excitedly. "With a horse trailer?"

"Honey, you're looking at the latest addition to the Mantler Circus. Ever hear of it?"

Danielle tried to think. "I think I remember seeing a poster in town last year."

Danielle's mom nodded. "That's right. I saw it, too. It showed a girl riding a horse while standing up on his back."

"You got it," Mrs. Loon said, pointing a finger at Danielle and her mom. "It's a small one-ring circus that tours the Northeast this time of year. Bareback riding, trained dogs, that sort of thing. And now, me and Dooley!" She smiled at Danielle.

"My ex-husband's sister is one of the bareback riders for Mantler," Mrs. Loon went on. "She called me in the hospital and said I should hook up with the circus when I got out. They were playing outside Miami and are heading up to the Washington, D.C., area."

"Sounds like a good gig," said Mr. Conners.

Mrs. Loon shrugged. "I could definitely use a break from the nightclub circuit." She turned back to Danielle. "And after your dad told me about your problem with your horse, I thought I could help out. We'll be going straight through Rocky Mount, I think. And my niece, Myra, is going. She's been working with horses all her life, honey. I'm sure she can handle your Redman."

This is too good to be true! Danielle thought.

"Even if your dad and I weren't old pals, I figure I owe you folks for looking after Dooley for me."

"You don't owe us a thing," Danielle's dad said.

The woman shook her head. "Oh, yes, I do. I know that bird. He can be a real handful."

Mr. Conners laughed. "Well, he's been quite an addition to the farm. And his wing has healed up just fine."

"Well, Danielle," Mr. Conners said. "Mrs. Loon has come to the rescue. Get Redman ready to go."

Mrs. Loon looked at her watch and nodded. "Myra said she'd be here with the van in about half an hour. That enough time, sweetie?" she asked Danielle.

"Uh, s-sure," Danielle said, still a bit stunned. Everything was happening so fast.

"I better start thinking about getting Dooley's travel cage ready, too."

"Thanks, Mrs. Loon," Danielle said, shyly. "I can't tell you how much this means to me. And to Redman," she added quickly.

"Don't thank me, honey," Mrs. Loon said. "You go get that paint ready. And don't you worry, I'll take good care of him and see that he gets where he has to go."

"Go on, Danielle," her mom urged.

Danielle ran out to the paddock, where Redman was waiting, and gave her horse a quick brushing. Mrs. Loon followed her a couple minutes later. Soon Dooley was crowing loudly as Mrs. Loon tried to corral him and get him into his travel cage.

A big white pickup truck pulling a horse trailer came rumbling up the driveway. A dark-eyed blond girl stepped out as soon as the truck stopped. She looked about eighteen, Danielle guessed, and was very pretty. The girl came over and gave Mrs. Loon a big hug. "Hi, Aunt Leslie," she said.

Too bad Alec is working with Raven, Danielle thought. *He would probably like to meet a girl like that!*

"Myra, dear," said Mrs. Loon. She glanced back toward the road. "Where's everyone else?"

"At a gas station, getting fueled up. They sent me to collect you all."

Mr. Conners helped Myra load Dooley's cage into the back of the pickup. Then Myra walked over to Danielle and Redman. "Hi," she said.

Danielle smiled nervously. "Hi."

"That sure is a good-looking paint," Myra said.

"Thanks. His name is Redman."

Myra reached up and gently rubbed Redman's neck. "Good boy," she said softly. "Are you ready to hit the road?"

The paint's ears pricked forward at Myra's words. Danielle felt a pang of jealousy. As if to reassure her, Redman turned to face Danielle and uttered a muffled neigh as his mane fell in front of his eyes. She brushed it out of the way and rubbed his forehead.

All at once, Danielle realized that this was it.

Redman was leaving. Again. *When will I be able to make enough money to buy Reddy back and bring him home for good?* she wondered.

"Oh, Reddy," she said, sighing. Her arms fell into place around his neck. "I'm gonna miss you so much." She pressed her head hard against the paint's forehead. The two of them stood there a moment silently. Finally, Danielle stepped back. "I'll get you the directions to Mr. Sweet's riding camp and the phone number," she said to Myra. "They're in my room."

The older girl nodded. "Okay, I'll start getting the van ready."

Danielle ran into the house and up to her room. Her address book was in her top drawer. She printed the information she needed on a piece of paper and returned the address book to the drawer. Then she glanced at the picture of Redman in the little gold frame on top of her bureau, choking back tears.

She promised herself that someday soon she would get the money together to bring Reddy home for good.

Danielle took a deep breath and remembered their last ride together that morning. *Hold on to that thought,* she told herself.

Pocketing the piece of paper with the directions on it, she ran down the stairs to say good-bye.

Redman loaded easily into Myra's horse trailer.

"Don't worry, Reddy," Danielle told him. "It's just for a little while. You'll be coming back. Soon. I promise." Redman bobbed his head as if in understanding. Danielle stepped outside the trailer and Myra closed the doors.

"Thanks again," Danielle said, handing the young woman the directions to Mr. Sweet's riding camp. "I owe you big-time for this, Myra," Danielle said seriously. "I won't forget it."

Myra smiled. "Hey, no problem."

"Let's get rolling, Myra," Mrs. Loon called.

Er-RUH. Dooley seconded the motion from his cage in the back of the truck. The two women jumped into their seats, and a minute later the truck and trailer were heading down the driveway.

Mr. and Mrs. Conners waved from the porch. "So long!" Mr. Conners called.

"See ya! Be safe!" Mrs. Loon called back, leaning out the window.

Alec had just finished his workout with Raven and was walking the colt back toward the barn. Danielle ran to meet them. Raven was sniffing the air as he watched the truck and trailer drive off. He tossed his head and whinnied sharply after Redman. "Where do you think *you're* going?" the colt seemed to be saying.

Danielle took a deep breath, fighting back her tears again. "Your buddy is leaving," she told the colt. "I bet you're going to miss him when he's gone."

"Happy trails, Redman! Keep on squawking, Dooley!" Alec called after the trailer, waving. Danielle started to wave again, too. She kept it up until the truck was out of sight.

Raven whinnied again. It was more of a lonesome, calling sound this time. Danielle stepped over to him and gave him a pat on the neck. The touch of the colt's warm coat made her feel better.

"Don't worry, Little Buddy," she told him. "We'll all be together again soon. You'll see, this is just good-bye for now. We haven't seen the last of Redman yet. I promise."

Have you read all the

YOUNG BLACK STALLION

books?

#1: The Promise

#2: A Horse Called Raven

#3: The Homecoming

#4: Wild Spirit

And coming soon:

#5: The Yearling (August 1999)

#6: Hard Lessons (December 1999)